I0581731

I, Ghost

A Paranormal Autobiography

Note from the author

The Paranormal genre is a departure from my other books. At times I struggled with it.

Everybody wonders about life after death. Religions all over the world claim to have the answer. Good behavior in life leads to a Paradise. Bad behavior leads to an eternity of torment. That sounds like the old carrot and the stick to me. Imagining Paradise is much harder than imagining Hell. Yet the descriptions vary tremendously.

I have been seeking those places for years. As an engineer, I applied logic, keeping myself free of the traditional teachings. I believe in this book. I nailed it.

I also applied logic to my Evolution River series, where I explore where the human race is going into the future. By the third volume in the series, thousands of years from now, I came to the end of evolution.

The saying is that nobody has come back after death to tell us about another life. I thought it was time to do so.

R. L. Clayton

Other books by R. L. Clayton
The Evolution River Series
Sea Species
The Envoy
Genesis

Wings of the WASP (a historical novel)
Penelope the Pooting Spider (a children's book)
The Dead Series
Dead & Dead For Real
Dead Reckoning
Dead Again
Risen from the Dead
Dead Prey
Dead but Not Gone
DeadWare
DeadSpace

I, Ghost

Visit R. L. Clayton's websites
www.rlclaytonbooks.com
www.evolutionriver.com

Comments

I had not expected to write a paranormal book, but my interest was tweaked by a member of our writer's workshop. I did not want to write a horror story. Yet I put horror and torture in this book. I have had a fascination with Edgar Cayce for decades. This seemed like a chance to throw out some ideas on America's Mystic.

My graphic artist, Steve Linebaugh, continues to produce great book covers, posters, newsletters, and artwork. He has created a number of videos that can be viewed on YouTube. He struggles to get me to participate in the promotion of my work. Keep the whip going, Steve. Links are on my website: www.RLClaytonbooks.com. We are having fun, Steve!

Acknowledgements

The writing community is amazing. We help each other out. We suggest, prod, edit and meet in order to make ourselves better. The editing group is an absolute necessity. Ted Dreisinger, Janet McCormack, and one of the best writers I know, Rosemary Simpson are all accomplished authors in their own right.

Steve Linebaugh is invaluable in creating my covers and artwork. His videos are great. Visit him at www.artbygordon.com.

Thank you all.

Prologue

My heart pounds at the clang of my cell door opening. My continuous pain is pushed into the background, replaced by fear. I squeeze my eyes closed to keep the glaring light away as I try to rise. My arms and legs refuse to respond. Rough hands grab me and drop me onto a gurney. Straps hold me down as the smell of urine-soaked sheets assails my nose. The wheels bump over the cracked and broken concrete floor with a clatter.

I know to keep my eyes closed. Looking at whoever is pushing me results in a sharp slap. The only sounds are the rattling wheels and the grunts of the pusher. The gurney turns and enters a room. It stops. The straps are loosened, and I'm placed on a table. I gasp as new straps are tightened until I can hardly breathe. Another strap acts as a blindfold and holds my head still. IVs are inserted in the portals in my arms, legs and neck.

I've been here before and begin to shake. It's waterboarding time.

I choke as water pours onto the dirty rag covering my face. My lungs begin to fill. I'm drowning. As I almost pass out, the water stops and the table tilts with my head down. I sputter and cough up water. I take a deep breath. The table tilts back, the water resumes.

How many times this is repeated, I don't know. I lost count, or maybe I just didn't bother. I finally pass out and awake to the darkness back in my cell. I have never been asked a question. It doesn't matter. Sometime during the electroshock torture, I told them everything I knew and made up what I didn't. Was it days…or weeks? I have no way of knowing. I am moved from one chamber to another to experience levels of pain I never knew existed.

The torture varies from electroshock to waterboarding to some drug that is injected and makes every nerve in my body scream as if I am on fire. I had been put into a freezer until I started to fall unconscious, then plunged into a warm bath. It felt as if I were being scalded to death. With all of this agony, not a mark is on my body.

I pray for my heart to stop and release me, but the man who inflicts my pain is an expert. He won't let me go.

I, Ghost

Chapter 1

Despite my torturer's best efforts, I can feel my life slipping away. I welcome the thought of release. My heart thuds irregularly in my chest. I am freezing cold, then burning hot. My body aches, then I am numb from head to toe. Death cannot come soon enough.

When my cell door clangs open this time, I sense I will not return. The touch of the rough hands on my skin is agony. I scream. The slaps on my face do not stop the shrieking. I no longer care.

"Shut up," yells somebody. It's a boy's voice, not the man I had heard before. Something is different.

In the electroshock room, I am strapped down tightly, pads are attached to my genitals, to my temples, to my chest. A probe is inserted in my rectum. My muscles knot at the thought of what is to come.

"Did I do it right?" asks the adolescent voice.

"Yeah," growls the one I recognize. Let me show you how to put the heart monitor on his chest and the EEG pads on his temples. Now we Insert the sampling IVs into the portals. We'll start light with low power. We have to be careful. Short bursts only. Watch that monitor. If his heart stops, we use the defib to kick it back on."

The man speaks in Americanized English with no accent I can detect. I had never heard enough speech from him to identify that before.

"Yeah, Okay, Dad. I got this."

I am somebody's lesson in torture.

A phone sounds. "Jon, I need to take this. Don't do anything until I get back." The door screeches open then bangs shut.

"I know what to do," mutters the boy.

Pain lances through me. My whole body

contracts until only my head and my heels are touching the table. I try to scream through the gag in my mouth. Unlike in the past, the shock doesn't stop. Something snaps within me, and I find myself floating above the table. I look down and see my body is still on it. Wisps of smoke drift up. A dark-haired boy has his hand on the switch. When he releases it, my body collapses in on itself but I remain in the air watching, as if viewing a movie.

The boy puts his hand to my throat. He stares at the monitor on the wall. His eyes grow wide. In a panic, he reaches for the defibrillator. He holds two paddles to my chest and steps on a pedal. Again, my body convulses, but this time I feel nothing as though I'm not there. He checks my pulse again. He shocks my body again and again. I remain above it all, watching.

The door clangs open and a man in a disposable coat steps in. He takes one look at me and runs to the defibrillator to check the settings.

"I...I didn't shock him that much," stutters the boy.

The man cuffs him hard enough to send him to

the stained concrete floor "I told you to do nothing!" the shout echoes in the room. The boy opens his mouth to speak, but a vicious kick in the face snaps his head back. The man turns back to my body. "Shit!"

He desperately attempts to revive me, but I'm not going back. The room begins to fade until I'm in a heavy fog. Everything is indistinct, like fuzzy shadows, the two people are like candles, glowing lights almost smothered by the haze.

I start to drift up, leaving this scene, this world behind. Fear of not knowing where I am going causes me to reach back, grasp at anything. My torturer is the last thing I saw, and it's him I strive to touch. He is like an anchor to my old reality and I hold onto this chain. It's there and I have it!

An invisible wind is pulling me away, but I hold to this string like a kite, swaying back and forth. I could let go and float away to…. I'm not sure where, but I want to keep the link to this reality, at least for now.

My eyes see nothing, my ears hear nothing. They remain with my dead body. It is my spirit that reaches out into the void that surrounds me. The two lights of the people weren't lights at all, but a glow, a sensation. My mind is linked with the man, my torturer.

The continuous pain I was subjected to buried everything else. I have no past, no memory, not even a name. Nothing before being here. How long ago was that? I would need a memory to know. This man was the only human contact I had after being…taken? Was I taken or did I volunteer for this? I don't know.

I will not let this link go.

He would speak to me kindly at times, but the sessions always ended with torture and pain. I try to remember my life, but can't. Perhaps it is buried under the scar tissue from the torture. Or maybe it was burned out of me. Only memories of pain and the cell remain. Who was I? This man became my tie to the past life, to the world I had left. Holding onto him is the only way I'll find out.

I feel the sensation of movement, though without distance or time, I have no reference. I know not where he is going, if anywhere, but movement is only an impression, and I am determined to maintain the link. The glow of the boy is faint, my sense of him weaker, but he accompanies the man. Other lights move past and around, but none hold my interest. I do not think any link could be established.

Another glow seems to join them. For a brief moment, they merge then move apart. I feel an emotion from him, a faint trace, nothing I can identify before it fades into the fog, like smoke.

His glow moves, then stops. I try to reach into him through the link, but everything is confused. Emotions and sensations play through him in a mad jumble, a rush like videos on fast forward all run together. I can latch onto nothing and am carried along like a leaf in a turbulent stream. The stream calms until I'm in still water. He must be resting. I hold the link tightly in my mind. I'm not ready to leave his world. I have things to do.

Chapter 2

I want to explore this new place I'm in, but I can only reach out with my mind. I'm not sure it could be called a place. I sense others but only like warm currents of air, brief sensations. I keep reaching out and encounter more minds, hundreds, maybe thousands. My reach is limited. They surround me but give no indication they are aware of my presence. Does each have a link to the world we came from? Are they even from that world?

I select a consciousness and focus on it, but there is nothing to grasp. At times, it seems to swirl around me, but disappears when I reach out. It is like something seen from the corner of your eye. But when you look, nothing is there. I'm frustrated but decide to stay with it. Maybe it will sense me in time. Nothing happens.

I move to another. This one is different, more active. The sensation is of a breeze around me, not hot, not cold but of movement. I allow myself to drift in the current of this mind, becoming passive like a leaf in a stream. There are ripples, like pebbles creating flows and eddies. I realize these are emotions. I focus on one.

I feel pride swelling inside me. It is from accomplishments, from high status, rank above others. This is obviously from the life this being has left. Yet it holds onto it. Is this a link like my own to the life before death? Does it choose to keep this link or is it a leash holding it here?

Will I be able to release my own link if I so choose? I wonder, yet to let that go is permanent. And I know not what lies ahead. I'm not afraid to let go, I have a task yet to perform from that past life. I drift into another current.

There is hatred within this one. It is a hard and cold emotion as if I am caught in an icy draft. The object of this hatred is a person, a rival. I imagine this emotion is similar to the one I hold for my torturer, though I have not examined myself. The hatred holds this mind like a powerful magnet, making it difficult to pull away. Does the link hold onto the mind or the mind onto the link?

Floating alone, I examine my connection. I hold onto it because it will be the only way I can exact revenge not only for the pain but for my past which he took. Yes, it is revenge I want to bring about against my torturer. Without any physical presence to my past life, I know not how I will do that.

I go to another mind, like moving into a cloud. Again, there are swirls of current, and I allow myself to be swept along. I feel love, powerful love that carries me. In her past life, somehow, I feel this is a she who loved someone completely. I feel concern for her, yet I also feel envy. This woman was not the main object of her loved one's affections. Her unrequited love lasted much of her life. The intensity grew and waned over the period of years, it never died. I feel her regret that her relationship was not intensified while it was new and strong. She blames herself for paths not taken.

Even after her life is over, she cannot let go. Her link is like a heavy steel collar she cannot remove.

I am jealous that these people have memories of their lives and I do not. I will make my torturer pay for taking that away.

As I move away from this, I consider another mind. This one is like a black fog. The hatred I sense comes over me like an all-encompassing weighted blanket. It is directed at everyone from his life, yet more powerfully toward himself. His link is to that lifeless body he has left, and like a spider's web, it spreads outward trapping everyone else, seeking revenge against the world. He was alone and always the victim, and cannot let go, for that defines him. I hurriedly move away for this feels like I am on fire, my soul burning.

If I were in my body, I would gasp in relief to be away. There are more minds to explore.

Chapter 3

Leon arose to the smell of breakfast cooking. He performed his morning ablutions, dressed in his black suit, one of many. His red tie was like newly spilled blood running down his chest. In the kitchen, his wife, Barbara, placed a plate of eggs with sausages and toast in front of him. As he sat, he glanced at his son, already seated at the table.

"Dad, I'm sorry about yesterday."

Leon felt a little remorse about the black eye the boy had. "I'll have to explain the death of my subject to my boss today. It won't be pleasant."

The boy's lips pressed together in a thin line as he looked down.

* * *

As Leon stepped from the bus, he stopped and stared at the huge windowless building. Everybody who worked there called it the Institute. It looked like nothing more than a concrete block three stories high and two hundred yards long. No hint of the underground rooms where the torture was administered. The walkway from the bus stop through the small parking lot led to a single door. No flowers, nor shrubs lined the sidewalk. No sign graced the outside telling what business was inside.

There was no hint of the depravity going on within. Perhaps he should quit, but the pay was too good. After this meeting, there might be no choice.

At the swipe of his badge, the door opened. He nodded to the guard in the atrium and approached the entrance door, inserted his ear bud and held his badge to the reader. He looked into the iris scanner. With a soft buzz, the door clicked open.

"Proceed to Section Manager Kwang's office," came a message.

The elevator started as soon as he entered. There were no buttons to push–it knew who he was and where he was going. My anxiety made this ride seem endless. The doors whispered open to the carpeted hall of the top floor. A petite woman in a traditional Asian dress of dark green silk ushered him into the First Manager's office. She closed the door as she left.

Manager Kwang stood behind his desk. He was small, also with Asian features. "Please sit, Mr. Prosky." He gestured to the straight-backed chair in front of the huge desk. "I understand we lost one of our subjects last night."

"Yes, sir. It was my fault. A moment of inattention."

"I have reviewed the video footage and see that there was a boy with you."

"Yes, sir. He is my son."

"Our rules here at the Institute regarding secrecy are quite specific. Employees are never to talk about their work, much less bring someone else in. How did you get him past security?"

"The guard had stepped away for a few seconds. We walked in under my badge."

"We'll have to take care of that."

"Sir, I was hoping to train my son so he could be considered for employment."

"Ah. Making your work a family business?"

"Yes, sir."

"That is admirable and a tradition from ages ago. Do you wish to continue with his training?"

"Yes, sir, if that is possible."

"We can do that, but in a more formal manner. How long have you worked in your present capacity?"

"My three-year anniversary is next month."

"You started soon after our operation began. Do you understand what we are doing?"

"I only know what I do."

"That is as it should be. Since you've been here three years, I will explain. We are a medical facility. The project you are with deals with the human body's production of enzymes and chemicals under extreme duress. A wide spectrum including endorphins and adrenaline are released into the bloodstream. Those are the common ones. Others not yet studied, even some not yet fully identified, are also present. What we are after actually doesn't fight pain directly. It triggers the body to release massive doses of pain fighting substances.

"We collect samples of those and hope to extract useful medicines from them that can be synthesized. At some point we will have the ultimate chemical control for pain, but also fear. Unfortunately for our subjects, we have not been able to isolate and purify the particular chemicals needed and thus must collect new samples continuously."

"Who are these subjects?"

"We have an arrangement with the criminal justice department to handle the execution of those found guilty of capital crimes. One thing we have found is that after several weeks of continuous *treatment*, their past is gone, burned out of them, so in a sense we have met our obligations. The bodies, though living, are now factories producing critical information and substances for the good of humankind. The loss of a subject will set us back, but not critically." He smiled.

Leon was stunned by this explanation. He had refused to speculate as to the reason for the torture, telling himself it was only a job. Did the ends justify the torture? He would have to think on this. The subjects were criminals sentenced to die anyway, and something good was coming out of their worthless lives.

Manager Kwang spoke. "I'm sure you remember how extensive the interview process was. You were chosen because you were able to follow orders. You had no sadistic streak and wouldn't particularly enjoy the pain you were inflicting on others, but you would do it. We rejected many other candidates as unsuitable."

"Thank you, sir, for the explanation. I was having trouble rationalizing my work. I feel better."

"Bring your son back and we will put him into the formal training program you went through when you started. We will assess if he is suitable for our needs."

The Section Manager rose, signaling the end of the meeting. Leon gave a slight bow and turned as the woman opened the door for him.

Chapter 4

The more I let go of myself when I am with another mind, the clearer its consciousness becomes. I feel like a thin stream of smoke twisting around another until it is one. I am aware of other minds around me. I reach out.

This one has a memory of its past life. I must have had a past but the pain from the torture has blocked me like a scar over a deep wound.

This man–I am sure it was a man in the other world–was wealthy and remembers the things he owned. He lived in a huge house, had expensive cars, and original artwork worth millions. He feels pride as he remembers the status he had, admiration and envy he enjoyed. His lifetime was spent building his achievements, acquiring things not because he enjoyed them but because they marked his rank and position. Yet he wasn't boastful to others.

The strongest memory is of the woman who was his wife. She was beautiful and enhanced his life by being kind and helpful to others. They had great love for each other. His loss of her is an intense ache. He is concerned she is unable care for herself now that he is gone. He hopes her grief period is not too long. He wants her to find happiness.

I feel myself carried away in his memories and embrace this idyllic and beautiful life. Did I have a past like that? I can only hope so. But how did I end up in a torture chamber? I would like to stay with him, but he clings to his past life and all he achieved. In this existence he has nothing but the memories, and they hold him in a firm grip. His inability to continue living that past life is painful. Unless he is able to let go, this is his hell.

I pull away and extend my mind to seek another to explore. If I had eyes the next spirit would be a glowing cloud. Instead, it feels like a warm spot in my mind. This one is in emotional agony; we have no physical bodies. It is a woman who had loved someone completely; he loved her back. Her life unfolds before me. From a family of three, she was the middle child. She had many friends in school but no romantic relationship until in her mid-teens. It was her first boyfriend; she fell hopelessly in love.

She had mapped out a whole life with him, but over time his ardor for her diminished until it was not returned. She desperately tried to bring it back, but nothing she did rekindled that fire. When he left her, she held onto that love and the life she had imagined. Unable to put it aside, it consumed her, figuratively and actually. She took her own life. Yet here she still longs for what she never had. What happened in her life saddens me terribly. That she carries that burden past death is tragic. Her death was not an escape from the misery of that life; only an entrance to another. Unless she is able to let go of that past life, here she will remain. I am relieved as I pull away from that sadness.

I seek another spirit and move into it. This merging is becoming easier. I recoil. This one is like a ball of snakes, writhing and twisting in a dark place. I want to withdraw, but am fascinated, hypnotized. It beckons me into an atmosphere that if I had a sense of smell, would reek. I build a shell to keep it out, yet I want to learn more.

This man was so warped by bitterness and cruelty he became the epitome of evil. I follow his life back to his childhood. The only attention he received was during the many beatings. He was berated and abused verbally and physically until he hardened and struck out at anything around him. His joy was in the torture of animals and those not able to stand against him. At the age of fourteen, the horrible home atmosphere drove him away to live on the street. He had to fight for everything. After repeated arrests ranging from theft to battery, he learned how to manipulate others and joined a gang.

They had staked out their territory for theft, burglary, extortion, drugs and prostitution. Success was short-lived when they ran up against the cartel controlling that territory. A war broke out resulting in the deaths of members of the gang and the cartel.

In the end, the resources of the cartel won. He was captured.

His ferocity in the battle earned him respect and he was given a choice to join or die–unpleasantly. He did not have to use his imagination to see what methods might be employed, he'd performed many of those himself. He joined. Within a year he became a *sicario*, a soldier. Again, his viciousness earned him a reputation, and he moved up. His number of killings rose. The man above him mysteriously disappeared, until his headless body was found hanging from a highway overpass. This man moved up to number two.

For most of those in the gang, money was the objective. Not for him. Power over others through fear and intimidation drove him. His loyalty to his boss was a sham to cover his plans to take over. He was discovered.

I knew the pain of torture, yet the intensity he suffered surprised even me. My torture was methods leaving little physical evidence. Not his. His death took days. Like me, we both held onto a tie to the past life for revenge.

As with me. his link was to his torturer, in his case, his boss. Without the ability to physically contact anything in his past life, he could do nothing, but he was able to influence his boss's mind. I wanted to learn that. I felt him insert visions and noises when he was asleep. His dreams were horrifyingly real as he reappeared. Sometimes his manifestation was his original appearance, other times it was his skinless and headless body, what he was like before he was hung from a highway overpass.

He rejoices in the terror caused by the image of his bodiless head as it calls out his name. Claw-like fingers reach for his boss. Accompanied by the smell of blood or decay or shit, he usually wakes screaming or in a cold sweat.

His ability to place visions in the mind of a living person fascinates me. Could other spirits do this? I go over the experience trying to remember what he did, the method to do that. Exhausted, I pull away. Unlike him, I vow to leave this place…but not yet.

Chapter 5

I am determined to try to connect with my torturer. I concentrate hard and try to imitate the things the last mind I visited was able to do. By focusing, my link grows stronger. Faint sensations become apparent. His mind is sluggish. He must be waking up. I am not yet able to tap into his senses, but I can tell he is hungry. I intensify my concentration. Other sensations gradually appear. Smell is just a whiff and sound like a faint radio signal that rises and falls. I am only just aware these sensations are present, but I am sure I will get better. No sight or sense of touch yet. All of these feelings are very dim. Are they his or mine imagined? I am almost able to smell his food and his hunger decreases. He must be eating, though I sense no taste.

The longer I maintain this contact, the stronger the tie, the more of him I feel. I cannot sense anything of the world on my own, only through him. It is like riding in a car. The world appears only through the window. I cannot interact with it, only observe, but I know I will be able to influence his senses eventually. In the place I am, nothing exists but the glow of other minds.

During the dim periods–I think when he is sleeping–I am able to gain more access to him. It's as if a shield is down or weakened, though I do not believe he is aware of me. The sensations are chaotic at times. I'm beginning to read his senses more clearly, yet they do not seem to be external. Is he dreaming?

I form a picture of myself being tortured trying to impress that image on his mind, but nothing happens. It will take time, but I have a lot of that.

* * *

The glow of his mind is brightening. Images form, but they are unclear and waver as if under water. His ears pick up sound. There is a roar like a waterfall, but in the background are other sounds. I cannot make them out. I must keep trying.

I keep pressing myself to remember what happened during my torture and before, but all I can recall is pain and the relief that darkness brought.

Did he ask me questions? Did I have information he wanted? I don't remember. I do remember electrodes were attached to my head and needles were in my arms. Why? At random times in my dark cell, my screams were played back to me, having been recorded. I didn't know if I was in the torture room or not, the pain arose within me. My voice became ragged from my shrieks joining the recording. I couldn't control it.

I do remember trying to starve myself to escape, but I was blindfolded, my mouth forced open and a tube rammed down my throat. A foul mush filled my stomach. Afterward, I tried to vomit it up, but that only resulted in a repeat until my throat was raw, my teeth were loose and blood was in my spittle. I ate and drank what was given to me. The overwhelming pain makes remembering hard.

R. L. Clayton

* * *

My host, I began to think of him as that, was moving around. Through him the world I left appeared. He used the bathroom, washed his face, shaved and did the normal things I assume I did before I was taken. He dressed. When he looked into a mirror, I saw him clearly for the first time. The only other time was at my death when he tried to revive me. My spirit rose, above the table, but that vision was a blur.

He seems to be average height, not heavy not thin. His hair is brown, his face has an appraising look as he examines himself. His eyes are black.

A woman is in the kitchen and through him I can smell food. Not the pasty stuff I remember–one of the few memories I recall–but real food. If I had a mouth, it would be watering. He says something, but I can't understand him.

He sits and a plate of eggs and toast is placed in front of him. He eats and I strain to try to take in the sensations of tasting the food. I can't, but I know with time and practice I will be able to. This is new, this link.

My host rises, says something, I can't understand the words, dons an overcoat and leaves. After a short time, he stops. Other people stand with him. A few minutes later, he hears a loud noise, and a bus stops. He boards and nods at several people, obviously other riders he meets regularly. He speaks to one. Again, I cannot understand what is said. Though I hear the sounds, they will not resolve into words.

I try to see through the window, but everything is unclear, like looking underwater. At times, buildings appear as large shapes. I recognize nothing. With no memory, how would I know if I'd been there before? My host gets off and begins to walk. He approaches a large concrete building. I can see no windows. No sign identifies the nature of those inside. As he enters, he swipes a badge which hung around his neck on a lanyard. A steel door opens. The door clicks behind him. An elevator opens and he enters. There are buttons for three floors up and two floors down. He pushes the bottom button. When the door opens, he enters a locker room.

It is empty. I have seen no other person since he got off the bus. He undresses, carefully hanging his clothes in locker thirteen, and dons a disposable suit from a stack.

He approaches another door and swipes his badge. The tiled shower room to one side smells of disinfectant and one shower head drips. He twists the faucet to turn it off, but it still drips. He shrugs and swipes his card again at another door.

I recognize the cracked concrete floor of the hallway and the smell. This was where I'd been tortured.

Chapter 6

My host, my connection to this life, walks into one of the rooms. I recoil as the scene brings up a memory. It looks exactly like the cell I was kept in. A woman is on the mattress in the corner. She is thin, her brown hair matted with grime. The long shirt she wears has traces of blood. She hides her face as my host approaches.

A heavyset man pushes a gurney into the room. A memory of my being strapped down on it rises in my mind. The woman shies away as the men reach for her. They pick her up as if she weighs nothing. A cry escapes her lips. My host, the torturer slaps her.

Strapped to the gurney, her chest heaves to silent sobs as he pushes her out, tears running from her tightly closed eyes. My host follows the rattling cart down the hall and into a room I recognize. Waterboarding.

I try to scream, try to stop this as she is moved onto the tilting board and strapped down. Electrodes are attached to her head and body, needles inserted into the ports on her thin arms. Like a mouse in a cage, I bounce around inside the host's head to make him stop. Nothing works. Helplessly, I watch her torture. The only sounds are her gagging and coughing up the water. No words are spoken.

When at last my host is done, the IVs and monitor pads are removed and her unconscious body is strapped onto the gurney. She is wheeled out, back to her cell, I presume. My host returns, showers and washes thoroughly, the paper suit is thrown away. At his locker, a note is stuck to the door.

Though blurry, I can read it. "See the First Manager when you are done."

After dressing, he grunts as he inspects himself in the mirror. Turning, he exits and takes the elevator to the third floor. This hallway has highly polished floors and wood-paneled walls. He pauses outside Section Manager Kwang's door. Taking a breath, he knocks.

"Come in." The voice is high-pitched. I'm surprised at being able to understand words now.

"Leon, take a seat," says a thin man dressed in a tailored black suit and bright red tie. He gestures to a chair in front of his desk.

I can feel my host's uneasiness as he sits.

"We've considered your desire to bring your son into the program. Though at seventeen, he is younger than any candidates we've considered before, we would like to give him a chance. He will have to be tested and examined to see that he is suitable. Pending a favorable outcome, you may mentor him."

"Thank you, sir. I'm sure Jon will be fine in the testing."

"I must tell you that his unauthorized attendance to a session has given him knowledge about our operations that should never have been allowed outside of this building and our employees.

We are considering the consequences if he is found unsuitable."

Leon's level of apprehension goes up another notch. The word *consequences* is disturbing.

"Bring him in tomorrow to begin the testing."

The director's smile seemed false, less than genuine.

* * *

Leon left the office showing more confidence than he felt. His son was young and impetuous, his actions resulting in the death of one of the company assets. If his rebellious attitude showed in the testing he could fail. Then what? *Consequences*. That word was a needle in his heart.

He tried to hide his worry from his wife and son when he arrived home. Tonight, he and Jon would spend time preparing. And his wife could know nothing. She would hover and disrupt the lessons. She would not understand there was no way to go back. His decision to take Jon with him had put them on a path with no exit, no room for failure. How could he have been so foolish?

* * *

I feel Leon's pain and concern, but I cannot share them. Though he had felt no pleasure in my torture, he had continued. He had been able to compartmentalize his actions and isolate them from the human feelings of empathy and compassion. I am determined to make him pay, though I am not sure how.

Chapter 7

Leon looked at Jon as they sit in his small study with the door closed. "Son, I made a huge mistake when I took you to work with me."

"What do you mean, Dad? I wanted to go. You never told me anything about your work, and I hounded you for the last year. I'm glad I went." He looked at the floor. "Sorry about screwing up. I just wanted to show you I could do it."

"You didn't feel anything for the poor man I was torturing?"

"Nah. I'm sure he deserved it, whatever he did. It was you dishing out punishment, right?"

Leon stared at the boy. "That project is ultra-secret. Nobody is supposed to know what goes on in that building." He shook his head. "And now you know."

"So?"

"I asked to bring you on as an employee." Jon whooped and pumped his fist in the air. "You have to pass an exam before you can start as my assistant."

"Easy-peasy. You know I can take tests."

Leon sighed. "It's not like any test you've ever taken before. It's a mental aptitude test, one to see if your attitude fits the position."

"I'm not squeamish about hurting people. I never told you, but sometimes I did things to animals, you know like Ms. Johnson's yapping dog."

"That dog disappeared. We assumed the coyotes got it."

He smiled. "Nope."

Leon closed his eyes. This was going to be hard. "Son, you can never tell anybody about that or let them think you enjoy causing pain."

"Why? It's what you do."

"I hate it, but it's my job and I do it."

"If you hate it, just quit."

"This is not a job one walks away from. That is why you must pass their exam. It's next week, and we have to get you ready."

"Why? What are they going to do, kill me?"

Leon fixed him with a silent stare. "And maybe me and your mom too."

Jon's mouth fell open. "You're serious aren't you?"

"Deadly serious."

* * *

I listen to this exchange. The pain Leon feels is bad. He has made an unthinking and an unforgiveable mistake. Leon could be a man without a conscience when he chose, but his son has the makings of a monster. And he is the one who killed me.

I reach out trying to contact his mind. It is a jumble. Ideas flash, thoughts jump from one thing to another. I have to withdraw. I do have a feel for him though. Maybe when he's asleep and calmer, I can connect.

The true torture of Leon is through his son.

* * *

Leon struggled to convey the attitude Jon had to portray. "You have to show the testers you have loyalty, trustworthiness, and the ability to follow instructions." The boy nodded. "You must convince them you can separate emotions and work. You cannot get emotionally involved in the job. You cannot reveal that you enjoy the work."

Jon nodded like a bobblehead doll.

"Here's a trick you might use. Put this rubber band around your wrist. Whenever you get excited or feel the rise of emotion, snap it. Just don't let them see it. They'll know you're hiding something. Here, let's try it."

He watched Jon put the elastic band on.

"Put your hands in your lap. Fold them so I can't see the band."

He observed the boy as he complied. "What did you feel when that man on the table was being tortured?" Leon watched Jon's eyes glisten. "Snap the band."

"Ow! That hurt."

"Are you a baby? Hide the band. Again. Don't show any reaction."

I watch them repeat this act until Jon is able to show no emotion. Leon emphasizes that this is a matter of life or death. Game time is over.

Chapter 8

I can sense the boy sleeping and reach out to him. Vague images of his dreams appear. They are not clear. It's like I'm underwater and the shapes move about in a chaotic cloud. A dark shape comes into focus as it comes nearer. It is his father and I sense fear. He tries to draw away, but he is restrained. His fear rises to panic and his mind twists and turns trying to get away.

He awakes, but the turmoil remains.

Through his eyes I see his darkened room. He rises and dresses. The house is quiet, his parents asleep. He tiptoes to the door and walks out into the night. In the brightness of the moon, I can see the street is deserted, the houses dark. A dog barks at his passing and I feel his anger grow. In his pocket is a folding knife. He runs his fingers over it as he thinks of hurting the dog, but he knows his approach would increase the barking. Someone might wake.

As he continues walking a cat runs in front of him. He lunges for it, grabs a leg, but the cat hisses and bites him, scratching his arm. He let's go. Nursing his hand and arm, he licks off the drops of blood. He continues walking, "Damn cat," he mutters. Explaining the injuries will be difficult. He'll have to keep them covered.

At the end of the cul-de-sac lights are on in one house. Quietly, he approaches, glancing from side to side to assure himself the residents of other houses are asleep. Staying in the shadows, he nears the side of the house and peeks in the lit window. It's a bedroom and a teenage girl in pajamas wearing earbuds is sitting on the bed. She rocks her head in time to music only she can hear, her shoulder-length blond hair flies about. Mesmerized, he watches. She stops. The music must have ended. A minute later she starts again, then rises and dances around the room, arms waving in the air.

Part of him wants to hear the music and join her in the dance, but a darker part is angry she's keeping it to herself, that she seems happy while he is so miserable. He visualizes opening the window and crawling through, taking out the knife and cutting her to make her share his misery. An erection grows. With the earbuds, she might not hear him, but she might see him as she dances. Might not.

But he won't. The risk is too great. He wouldn't get to her before she would scream. Others would come.

After watching a while longer, he creeps back to the street. His anger has abated. Turning toward his house, he feels calmer. These walks at night help dissipate the fear and anger he feels. But he wouldn't forget the girl.

At his house, he sneaks back to his bedroom silently so as to not wake his parents. They will never know about his nighttime stroll. Lying in bed, he closes his eyes and the dancing girl appears. He smiles as he falls asleep.

I have no doubt he will try to hurt that girl, given the opportunity.

What can I do?

His mind is calm. I push an image of my body as I lay dying on the torture bench into his mind. He sees it.

His mental smile is not the reaction I expect.

Chapter 9

I am with Jon as he awakens to his father's voice calling him to breakfast. He goes to the kitchen, his head, fuzzy from lack of sleep due to the late night,. "Hey, Dad."

"Eat your breakfast and get dressed. I'm taking you to work with me. It's your test day."

"Great!"

"If you remember everything we talked about last night, you'll do fine."

Jon glances at this mother. She frowns and turns away to clean the breakfast cookware. Jon knows she doesn't approve of his trying to follow in his father's footsteps. She had babied him, trying to make up for the lack of attention he'd gotten from his father. He'd been mercilessly teased at school about being a mama's boy until he'd ambushed one of his tormentors and put him in the hospital. They'd kicked him out of school when he refused counseling. His mother's attitude toward him began to shift with his surly actions toward her.

Though he didn't know any details about his father's work, he senses both parents are afraid something will be revealed. It's a dark secret he doesn't understand.

His home schooling is mediocre despite his mother's best efforts. He goes through the motions with no enthusiasm. His poor grades during his quarterly testing is of no concern to him. He feels he's good at taking tests, but his scores belie that. His mother becomes exasperated at his failure to apply himself and learn basic schooling. In her frustration, she calls him stupid and dumb. He is not, just not interested. She became harsher in her instruction. Friendless, he withdraws into himself, bitter at the world and how it treats him.

* * *

He and his father get off the bus and walk to the concrete building. Jon is amazed by the size of the structure. At the reception desk, his father explains to the guard Jon is a candidate for testing. He is given a badge on a lanyard.

"Take him to the admin floor," instructs the guard.

A woman walks them to the elevator. "Get off on floor two. Tell the receptionist your name."

At the second floor, a woman smiles as they get off the elevator. "This must be Jon." She takes his hand. "I'll take him in and call you when he's done. It will be several hours." Jon glances back at his father as she leads him through a door behind her desk.

The room is nothing like any of the other places he's taken tests before. There are only two chairs and a coffee table. To one side is a desk with a few papers and a computer. Only diplomas and awards hang from the walls–no pictures or anything personal. A man in a suit and tie rises from behind the desk. He is thin, Asian with a stiff erect posture, black hair and black eyes. He doesn't smile or offer his hand.

"You are Jon." He gestures toward a chair. "I am Dr. Yoon. We're going to have a discussion about you, but don't be nervous. I want to get to know you, so just relax.

Kind words. Not what he expects. The man's face shows no expression as Jon sits in the chair in front of the desk. Behind the desk, he sits and glances at a tablet.

"Jon, this is an interview for you to apply for work here." He pauses and smiles, but it doesn't extend to his eyes. "What activities do you like?"

His dad had told him what to say. "I'm home schooled, so I study a lot."

"You don't study all the time, do you?"

"I read. Sometimes I watch movies at home."

"What kind of books do you like?"

"I like science fiction and thrillers–adventure stories." He had read a few.

Yoon nodded. "Give me an example."

"I like a lot of Isaac Asimov books, and the *Ender's Game* books."

"What movies do you like?"

"I like the *Alien* series and the first and second *Terminator* movies. Didn't care for the third or the others much."

"Did you find them scary?"

Jon was ready for this question. "Yes, but they were movies. It wasn't real."

"What about *Star Wars*?"

"I like all of those movies."

"Who is your favorite character?"

"Darth Vader," he blurts out. He'd watched the movies for the first time last week. The week had been filled with answering his dad's questions and learning about things other kids did.

Yoon stares at him for a second and makes a note on the tablet. "What sports do you like?"

"I don't really like sports much."

"What about friends?"

"Between my studies and my reading, I don't have a lot of time for friends."

"Do you have any pets?"

"We had a dog when I was young."

"What happened to it?"

"He died. Got hit by a car."

"How did you feel about that?"

"It made me real sad, hurt for a long time."

"Did you get another dog?"

"No. I wasn't going to get hurt like that again."

The testing goes on for a long time and becomes tiring. Often, the questions are repeats but phrased differently. He has to be careful.

At last, Dr. Yoon stands. "Thank you, Jon. We'll let you know in a few days about working for us."

The woman who had shown him in appears at the door.

Chapter 10

Leon came into the house and went to the kitchen. Jon was sitting at the table with a can of soda. Leon sat across from the boy.

"Well, how'd it go?"

Jon shrugged. "Okay, I guess. They said they'd let me know in a few days."

"How do you think it went?"

"They asked me question about my past, friends, pets, school–stuff like that. It was different from any test I've had before."

"Was the man questioning you smiling when you left?"

Jon looked down at the table. "Dad, his face was like stone. He never smiled or frowned."

Leon stared at Jon for a while. "I want you to pack a *go bag*."

"What's that?"

"Take one of your gym bags and put a change of clothes, set of sweats, spare toothbrush, toothpaste, bar of soap, towel, and anything else you think you'll need if you're not here. I'll get you some money and another phone. Keep that bag in the closet. If you have to leave, you can be gone in less than two minutes."

Jon's mouth gaped open. "You're serious, aren't you?"

"Lethal. I hope it doesn't come to that, but it's best to be prepared."

"What about you and Mom?"

"I've had a *Go bag* for a long time. I have a storage container with a lot of stuff. We can hang out there for a few days. I'll leave you the entry codes and a key in your bag. If the company decides you don't fit in, I'll try to convince them you ran away and I don't know where you've gone. If that doesn't work, we'll be leaving too. I'll put our phone numbers into your directory. We can meet at the storage site."

"Wow! This is like a movie."

"Unlike a movie, I don't hold out a lot of hope for the good guys. These are just precautions, but there is no reason not to be prepared."

* * *

Jon can't sleep, his mind a jumble. I am able to read his thoughts and sense his fear. I had been with him during the test. He thought he was prepared, but this wasn't a test like any he'd taken before. It was a conversation and the answers he gave were as important as how he said them, his voice, what words he used. He got no feedback from the man sitting across from him. His face was frozen like ice. Not even his eyes revealed anything as he stared at Jon, watching. He listened and entered notes on a tablet. Jon is sure it was all videotaped, though he saw no cameras.

After several hours of tossing and turning, he gets out of bed and dons some dark clothes. His neighborhood walks usually help him go to sleep. His house is silent as he slips out the door. Clouds cover the sky and the air is warm and heavy, promising rain. A block away, he is startled as a dog barks. He should have remembered. He reaches into his pocket for the folding knife but brings his fisted hand out empty. No, he won't risk it.

The house with the girl is completely dark. He slips up to her window and peers in. Her curtains are drawn. He sees nothing. Anger rises within him. Why is everything against him? Drawing his hand back to smash the glass, he freezes. Not tonight.

The warm splat of the first raindrops causes him to jump. He needs to get home.

Chapter 11

I had been with the boy as he had gone out the previous night. I felt his rage at having no control. It was the feeling of being a victim that drove him to hurt others, people and animals. I understand but hold no pity for him. He killed me.

My tie to the material world now has two strings, one to his father and one to him. I am getting better at entering their minds and reading them. I'm not sure why I feel this affinity for him.

* * *

Leon, the boy's father, had not slept well either. He was concerned about the results of the test Jon had gone through. He'd spent the night planning for the worst. Having to run.

He had searched his mind for a location where they were unknown and could resettle. Most of his life had been spent here except for his time in the army.

He'd been stationed at Ft. Huachuca in Arizona where he'd had a military career in computer and electronic hardware repair. Never rising above the rank of corporal, he was good at his work, but unambitious. He was smart enough to make grade, but the regimented military life was distasteful. He did the minimum amount to stay out of trouble and was glad to leave. The military made it easy.

Maybe a move to Arizona. The winters were pleasant, the spring and fall short and the summers pure hell.

* * *

As soon as Leon checked in at work, a note appeared on his tablet to report to Section Manager Kwang's office. He felt his stomach knot. As the receptionist showed him into the office, Mr. Kwang stood, leaned across his desk and shook Leon's hand. He smiled.

"You remember Dr. Yoon from your interview."

Leon turned and shook Yoon's hand. His memory of the man was vague.

"Please sit." Kwang gestured to the chair. "Dr. Yoon and I have looked over your son's test results. Though there are a few areas of concern, we would like to have Jon start training with us. He will go through a series of aptitude tests to determine the best area for his talents and interests. Tomorrow he will go through the introduction and safety procedures." He smiled again. "How does that sound?"

"Thank you, sir for this opportunity for Jon. I'm sure he will prove to be an excellent employee."

"My receptionist will give you the forms we need to have Jon fill out. You can bring them in with Jon tomorrow."

Leon recognized the dismissal. He headed for the door.

"Please emphasize again to Jon the need for secrecy. Nobody is to know of his work."

Leon turned back as he opened the door. "Yes, sir, I will."

* * *

As the door closed, Yoon turned to Kwang. "Of course, we will observe Jon carefully as we would with any new employee. The boy's badge has a tracker and monitor. We'll have cameras and a drone watch him for a while when he's not here where the CCTV will lock onto him. We will place microphones in his house when the opportunity arises."

"Leon will be monitored more closely," said Kwang. "He has been an exemplary employee, but when it comes to a father-son relationship we need to be vigilant."

"The boy seemed fine, but I could tell he'd been coached. A few things caught my attention. Nothing serious, but a little worrying. We'll see."

"And if he is not the employee we want?"

"Yoon shrugged. "That is always the concern."

Chapter 12

The rest of Leon's day seemed to drag as he wanted to tell Jon the good news. Working together would be the start of a relationship he'd missed. It was a second chance.

The waterboarding session with his present assignment was nearly over. The woman was unconscious and ready to be moved to her cell. She was proving to be quite strong. Leon removed the IVs and called his assistant to take her back.

He sped through the decontamination process and dressed. As the bus neared his stop, he became excited. He practically ran the short distance to his house.

"Jon," he called. "I have some good news!"

The boy looked up from his studies. "Hey, Dad. You're home early."

"You've been accepted at the institute. Fill these out." He handed the forms to Jon. "You can go in with me. They'll start the training program tomorrow. It'll take a couple of days and then you can be my apprentice."

"That's great, Dad." He got up and gave Leon a hug.

Leon was startled. He couldn't remember the last time Jon did that. It felt good. "We'll go out to dinner to celebrate. Where would you like to go?"

"I haven't had pizza since I was going to school. They served it sometimes. Let's get pizza."

* * *

I can feel their happiness. I hate it. Celebrating the creation of a torturer is wrong. Jon had been a torturer before, but this was formalizing it. Tonight, I will try to tarnish the moment.

* * *

Jon was so excited he wasn't able to go to sleep for hours. He could stand it no more and rose to take a walk. He dressed in dark clothes and tiptoed out of the house. The neighborhood was fast asleep. Even the dog who usually barked at him was silent.

The house at the end of the street where the girl lived was dark.

Jon looked at her window longingly, but the drapes were drawn. He heard a slight hum. Not from the house. He looked around, but could not locate the source. It was too faint. Maybe it was his ears. Not a problem. The night was cool but this walk had calmed him. Time to go home.

* * *

Just as Jon is about to drop off to sleep, I project the image of me dying on the electroshock table. I scream into his brain.

Jon jumps from the bed, stumbling as he tries to stand. He sprawls on the floor. I could feel his heart pounding. He is gasping for air.

Try to get back to sleep now you little shit!

I did it! Projecting into his mind worked. It takes effort on my part and I need to rest. I drift in the void.

* * *

"Son, didn't you sleep well?" asked Leon at the breakfast table. "You look tired."

"I'm just excited about going in with you," Jon lied. He didn't want to say anything about his nightmare.

"Finish eating and we'll go."

The boy forced himself to eat the eggs and sausage his mother had prepared.

* * *

Jon felt as if he was back in school except he was the only student. The class was human anatomy. He was having trouble staying awake during the slide show. On the screen was the nervous system. It looked like a roadmap. Why did he need to know this stuff?

Dr. Yoon's voice came over the speaker. "Wake up, Jon!" His head jerked. "There will be tests. Perhaps we will proceed to the model session. Use the Virtual Reality headset." Jon put on the goggles after adjusting the straps and picked up the hand sensors. "Stand up."

He was in a room with black walls and no windows. A spotlight illuminated a figure from the darkness. It was a human body. The skin had been removed leaving the musculature exposed. He had heard of a touring exhibit about the human body. It used real bodies preserved in various stages of dissection.

Yoon's voice surrounded him. "Walk around it, study how the muscles are attached to the bones. Muscles can contract to move the skeleton about the joints. Everything is labeled. Do try to remember the main ones. Study this exhibit closely. Take all the time you want."

Jon stepped close. He reached toward it. In his view, his hand clasped the arm of the body. He raised it and watched the muscles move. He moved the arm in a circle and saw the muscles that would perform that action stretch and contract. This was amazing. It was so smooth and detailed he couldn't tell it was an animation.

"We'll start with the skeleton." Only the bones were visible, an erect skeleton. "Remove them, examine them and replace them. Remember the names."

He spent several hours studying, taking even the smallest bones out. When he was done, he stepped back.

"Do you think you know the skeleton now?" The bones collapsed into a pile. "Rebuild it. Read the label and call out the name of each bone as you place it on the skeleton."

Jon moved forward and started with the feet. He continued up the legs. If he attempted to put a bone in the wrong place, it clattered to the floor. If he left bones out from one section, he was not allowed to proceed to the next until it was complete. After hours, the skeleton was complete.

"We will repeat this lesson until you can do it. in less than an hour without the name labels. Go home and get some rest."

"Why do I need to remember the name of each bone?"

"It's not the names of the bones that are important, it's your memory you must force to work."

The room disappeared. He was back with Dr. Yoon. He removed the headset and left. He was exhausted, but exhilarated. This was new and exciting.

Chapter 13

I felt Jon's excitement about his anatomy session. I was too exhausted to ride with him during the session, but as he replayed it at dinner, I could see this amazing equipment. "Dad, it was like going inside a person. I toured the skeletal system. I'll do that again tomorrow until I learn it."

"Three years ago, when I went through the training," said Leon, "they didn't have that system." I had to study from books and photos. The development of that medical program is another company department. They plan to sell the system to medical schools."

Why did this company require medical training for its people? I knew the answer as soon as the question arose. In order to extract the substances they wanted, the torturers, needed to know how to maximize the production of the human body during extreme pain and yet keep the subjects alive. The goal was admirable, the activity was monstrously evil.

I was able to get into the heads of first Leon and then Jon, but could I do that with others I've had no contact with? Only way to find out is to try. Tomorrow, I would need to ride Jon during his lesson. It would give me contact with his teacher. In the meantime, I would enter Leon tonight.

* * *

Leon lay in his bed staring into the dark and thinking of the education Jon was getting. He wanted that. Properly learned, he would have the ability to be a doctor, or at least a healer. Those skills could prove useful someday. Perhaps he could request that training tomorrow. Time for sleep tonight. He rolled over and closed his eyes.

* * *

As Leon was sleeping, I entered him and projected a vision of my body on his table. He felt sadness at my death, but not for me. As he looked,

I raised my arm and pointed at him. My mouth opened in a scream. Leon awoke and tried to push those images back into the box where he kept the horrors. I would not let him. Even though he was awake, I forced the scene of my body back on him. I rose and reached for him.

He jumps from the bed, all vestiges of sleep gone. In the kitchen, he pours himself a shot of whiskey, his hands shaking enough that as much spills onto the table as in the tumbler. He downs the liquor at once, feeling the burning from his throat to his stomach. I let him calm down.

I need to get into that box.

* * *

I stay with Leon in the morning. His night had been restless, his sleep not good. He accompanied Jon to the classroom. Dr. Yoon was waiting.

"Ah Jon, glad you're here. Good morning, Leon. Is there something I can do for you?"

"Dr. Yoon, I would like to take the lessons also. When I began working here several years ago, this marvelous equipment wasn't available."

"It is an amazing teaching tool. I'll speak to Mr. Kwang. Perhaps you could take the lessons in your off hours."

"Thank you, sir."

* * *

Yoon looks sternly at Jon. "Today you will repeat the skeletal system. Put on the headset and take up the controllers."

Eagerly, Jon adjusts the headset. He is back in the dark room. The light illuminates a human skeleton. He circles it, leaning in to closely to inspect the bones. They are labeled with the names. He pulls a rib out and hold it up, runs a finger along its length. He puts it back. It attaches itself.

"Study it," says Yoon's voice. "Take it apart, lay out the bones. Look at each, then put it back together."

Jon complies.

"Good, now do it again." The skeleton was again a pile of bones. Do it five times. Each time the light will become dimmer so you remember where things go and can assemble it in the dark by the feel of the bones."

Chapter 14

I stay with Leon, though I get a "taste" of Yoon. It is not enough to enter, but I will see more of him.

* * *

Leon is having trouble concentrating. At my prodding, the dreams from last night keep rising. He looks down at the poor woman strapped to the electro-shock table. Her eyes are closed as he inserts the IVs, attaches the monitors, the shock pads and probes.

Leon is like ice. No thought of the woman enters his brain. He is doing a job. Nothing more. Completely mechanical. My only contact with the physical world is with the senses of those I am in. Through his eyes, I watch the victim writhe on the table as electrical current pass through her. The gag prevents her screams from deafening Leon. He is actually whistling.

If I had a stomach, I'd be retching. As the torture continues, Leon checks the IVs and the vials they as they fill. He watches the monitors until her heart stops. He cuts the current and uses the paddles to restart her heart. He gives her a few minutes to recover and starts again. I follow the trace in his mind as he puts the whole scene into his mental box. He locks it.

But now I know where to find the key.

* * *

I am exhausted after pushing Leon and following Jon. I drift in darkness. The faint glow of other minds is the only thing that breaks endless darkness. I want revenge for the torture Leon put me through and for my murder by Jon. With any ability to connect with the physical world taken from me, how can I extract retaliation? I have learned to connect with their minds. I have also learned to create images and sensations in their minds. That will be my avenue for payback.

But now that I've been with them, I see them as people moved by circumstances and those around them. Certainly, what they did and continue to do is evil, but it's not just them. It's the attitude that victims aren't people but mere objects to be used.

The world had not moved past that attitude. I am beginning to remember more of the life I came from. Wars are the ultimate use of people as tools, their lives without meaning. Those in charge profess they care, but their actions belie that. Humanity hasn't changed since it came to Earth.

Leon is no different. Jon is at a stage where he can become truly malicious, relishing the pain of others. Can that be changed? It will eventually lead to his destruction. Do I want to change him?

Chapter 15

"What have you seen in our new recruit so far?" Kwang asked Yoon.

"The boy has exceled at the anatomy lessons. I have no doubt he can replace all of the parts into a complete human body. He studies and repeats taking the models apart and replacing them until he understands the make-up. He can to see the structure. We'll start his lessons with the musculature system next. As with our plan for medical students, the nervous system will follow, then the organs, the circulatory and the lymph system, the digestive system. We'll end the systems with the brain. He could be ready for diagnosis and treatments within three months."

"That's pretty fast. You're saying he might become valuable on the medical staff?"

"Yes. perhaps more so than the extraction team."

Kwang thought for a moment. "I sense there is more to consider."

"The boy has little social life, so he has no one to tell about our Institute. That is good. He is a loner. I wasn't able to get him to open up much about his childhood. I suspect he suffered some abuse. From his mother it may have been a combination of physical and verbal. Physical when he was younger, verbal as he grew up. From his father, it was mostly being ignored. This has made him an extreme introvert."

"What about school?"

"He has been home-schooled. Several incidents occurred in the public school. I checked records. After he severely injured another student, he was asked to not come back. His parents sought counseling for him, but couldn't afford it."

"What dangers do you see in him?"

Yoon glanced at the widescreen on Kwang's office wall. It was cycling through great art works, each painting showing for ten seconds. He looked back at Kwang. "He has trouble sleeping. Nightmares, I think. Late at night, he walks the neighborhood. He knows which houses have dogs and avoids them. Barking could wake up the owners. One house on his street in particular draws his attention. A young girl about his age, seventeen or so, lives there, He watches her."

"Is that a problem?"

"Not yet. But like a kid looking through the window of a candy store, at some point he may want a taste."

"Has he made any move to interact with her, talk to her?"

"He rarely goes out during the day, almost never farther than his back yard."

"Intriguing. Let's keep an eye on him. If you find anything that could be a danger, let me know. We'll discuss what to do."

"Yes, sir."

"What do you think about the father's request to go through some of the medical program?"

Yoon paused before answering. "I like the idea. It would be a good test of our program as he's shown little talent in the medical area. He does know how to inflict pain and extract the substances we want. His subjects last a long time, and that is a talent in itself."

"I agree. Let's see if our program is good enough to train someone with no particular aptitude toward the medical field."

"His sessions will be after his normal work schedule?"

"Yes."

"I'll set it up, sir."

Chapter 16

I have sensed a change in Jon. The medical training has caught his attention. He genuinely wants to learn more. The dark side of him has been supplanted by this new interest. I have slowed my injection of nightmares into his mind. He sleeps better.

Instead, I have increased the dreams Leon experiences. What he does is evil, and he should experience consequences from it. The first images of my body rising from his table and reaching for him now include muffled wails and cries. He is losing sleep.

* * *

I am riding with Leon after work as he waits for Dr. Yoon, whose office is empty except for a desk and two chairs. No diplomas adorn the walls, no pictures on his desk. The man enters, smiles and sits across from him

"I commend you on wanting to try the medical program. You are the oldest and the first non-medical person we've tried this with."

"What do you mean?" asked Leon.

"We're still testing it with a few university medical students. As you know, the program has not been released yet." He looks at his iPad. "We'll start with the anatomy classes." He hands Leon the VR headset.

I reach out for Yoon but my connection is too weak to sense him.

"Let me help you adjust the straps," Yoon offers. "The anatomy session is based on an exhibit that toured the country for several years. Perhaps you heard of it. It consisted of real bodies that were dissected and preserved. These allowed the visitors to view all aspects of the human body."

"I did hear about it. My wife thought it would be gruesome."

"Learning about the body can seem that way to some. We start with a skeleton to study bones.

Another lesson has the muscles attached but the skin removed. After that is one with the organs. We have succeeding lessons with the nervous system, the circulatory system, the lymph system, and the digestive system. The final lesson about the body is the brain. We have enhanced these visions in the virtual world and made it an interactive experience. You will be able to see the body, walk around it and various parts to examine more closely. The parts are labeled so you will learn the names.

"When you are able to disassemble a body and reassemble it, you will be ready to move on to the next series of lessons. I will be here, so if you need to stop, let me know."

Leon enters the viewing room. An erect skeleton stands under a spotlight, bones gleaming. He walks around it, leaning close to peer at one bone or another.

"Go ahead, Leon, remove a bone and examine it."

He takes an arm bone. It is labeled *Ulna*. It is smooth to his touch. He puts it back. He takes the hand and wrist as a unit. There seems to be dozens of small bones, and he holds it up to the light, turning it one way then another.

I can sense his fascination at being able to take any of the bones from the skeleton, look at them and put them back. He spends hours.

Suddenly, the skeleton collapses in a jumble.

"Reassemble it, Leon." Yoon's voice seems to float around him.

Three hours later, the skeleton stands before him, but about fifteen bones lay on the floor.

"I didn't get them all," Leon apologizes.

"It's okay. Pick one up."

He does. An area on the skeleton flashes. He places the bone there and it stays. He quickly reassembles the rest. He is exhausted, but he admires what he's done.

"You did well for the first time. Tomorrow we'll do this again. Remove the headset and go home. You need some rest."

* * *

The virtual reality session had taken a lot of energy. By the time he reached home, he couldn't keep his eyes open. Barbara had a reheated meal ready for him. He hardly tasted the food. Jon sat with him, his eyes glowing from excitement.

"What did you think, Dad? It was really cool, wasn't it."

"It was quite an experience. I understand why you liked it."

"The skeleton was easy. Tomorrow I start with the organs. Some of them are really small."

A part of Leon was jealous that Jon seemed to pick these things up so easily, but he was so tired Jon's voice faded away. He caught himself before his head hit the table. "I have to get to bed. I'll see you in the morning." He stumbled toward the bedroom.

I decide to let Leon sleep tonight. Tomorrow I will *help* with his next lesson.

Chapter 17

Jon slips out the door into the darkened neighborhood. He shivers as the memory of his dream floats before his eyes. A dog barks as he strolls toward the end of the street and the house where the girl lives. He stares at the sound of the barking. *I have to take care of that mutt, but not tonight.*

The curtains on the girl's window glow, lit from within, the only light coming from the house. She is awake. He looks both ways on the street. It is empty. While he watches, the light inside goes out. He creeps across the lawn toward the house.

The light comes on. Jon stops. It blinks off. He takes a step. It comes on again. He freezes. What's going on? The window is dark again. He takes another step. The light comes on.

I am enjoying Jon's confusion as he slowly backs away. He turns and runs toward his house. The dog barks again, and others join until the whole neighborhood sounds like a pound. *That's not right. I got rid of those dogs months ago.*

Inside his house, he leans against the door gasping, his heart pounding. After several minutes, he creeps back to his room and lies down fully clothed. His heart still hammering against his chest. The image of the man who had died in his father's room floats above him. His scream freezes in his throat.

* * *

Why had I stopped Jon? Was it because he might get caught or because he might not? Why do I have this attachment to him? It is more than the fact he killed me. Something in him seems familiar. I knew he'd go to the girl's house. I knew he'd killed several of the dogs in the neighborhood. I knew he was into himself above all else.

* * *

Leon felt like a million dollars as he sat at the table for breakfast. He'd had a good night's rest, his first in a week. *It's amazing what that will do for a guy.* "Where's Jon?" he asked.

"Hasn't come in yet," Barbara answered.

Leon went to Jon's bedroom. The boy was on the floor, wrapped in the bedding.

"Jon, get up." He nudged him with his foot. "You'll miss the bus. Being late is something they don't like at the Institute." Jon's eyes were red, his hair a mess. "Why are you on the floor?"

"I had a bad dream. I had an accident."

Leon glanced at the bed. The bedwetting signs were unmistakable, the smell of urine assailed his nose.

"Goddammit! What's wrong with you? You haven't done that in years."

The boy rubbed the spot where Leon's foot had connected with his ribs. "It was just the dream. I'm okay."

"Shower and get dressed. I'll get you something you can eat on the bus."

In the kitchen, Leon explained to his wife that Jon had had an *episode*. That's how they referred to the bedwetting before Jon outgrew it. "Fucking kid is reverting back. I won't take it, you understand?"

"Is he going to be all right? Is this work at the Institute the cause?"

He turned to find Jon standing in the doorway staring at the floor. When he looked up, there were tears on his cheeks.

"You'll be fine. We'll talk more about it at lunch."

Chapter 18

I have been trying to explore this place I am in. At first, it seemed almost empty, but I've become more sensitive. My mind reaches out. Now I feel like a grain of sand on the beach. Billions more are here. Some, like me, have ties to people from their lives that keep them in this place. Most wear their past like an overcoat, clutching it to protect themselves from something unknown. Yet, what they grasp are memories, thoughts of material things, status and control, power over others. Those don't exist to them anymore.

Few of them are able to connect with others. Or maybe they don't try. They drift alone. There are no happy souls here. The descriptions of streets of gold and twenty-nine virgins are lies to attract followers. The fires of hell are also a lie meant to beat them into obedience. Purgatory is where I am.

I now realize that to escape, I have to release all thoughts of my past life, take off the overcoat. But I'm not ready to do that. My hatred for my torturer holds me. I do wonder what my past life was like, but without a memory of that, it is one less thing I have to forego. Is that good or bad? I don't know. Are there second chances, opportunities to try life again and do better? Or is this eternity?

I do know the Institute and what they are doing is wrong. Am I able to do something about it? With my only avenue the ability to enter some minds, any influence on the world is limited. Yet I will try.

Why do I care? I am no longer in that world. Some part of me wants to do something right. *Drop it. Move on.* I can't.

Chapter 19

I ride along as Leon enters Yoon's office for his second lesson. Yoon awaits. Again, I try to connect with him. A small crack appears in his persona. I try to wriggle in but it closes before I get far. He shakes his head as he hands the VR headset to Leon.

"We're going back to the skeleton again. Become familiar with the bones by feel because the last session in this lesson will be done in the dark."

Leon dons the headset as I move fully into his mind. The skeleton appears before him again.

"When you remove a bone, put it on the floor," said Yoon. "When it is completely disassembled, I will dim the lights. Call out the name of each bone as you reassemble the skeleton."

Leon begins. He is doing well until he sees the toes of the skeleton wiggle. He yelps and jumps back.

"Are you all right?" asked Yoon.

"Did you see that?"

"See what?"

Leon clamps his mouth shut. This is in his head. He knows that. He also knows he can't reveal he is having hallucinations. "Nothing. My eyes played a trick on me. That's all." He continues with the bones.

He assembles the wrist and hand, then tries to place it on the arm. It waves about as if trying to elude him. He tries to follow it. Failing that, he grabs the arm and puts the assembly on it."

Inserting these illusions into Leon is fun for me, not so much for him.

"Leon, what are you doing?"

"I think something's wrong with the adjustment straps on my headset." He tightens them. He finishes the assembly without more incidents.

"Dr. Yoon, I'm not feeling well. Perhaps I should go home."

"Fine. Take off the headset and go ahead. I'll see you tomorrow."

* * *

"Dad, you're home early," said Jon from the table. He was doing homework.

Since he's started the lessons at the Institute, his studies have improved. He whips through his assigned homework in an hour and starts reading a medical text he's gotten from the library.

"I wasn't feeling well. Couldn't concentrate. What are you working on?"

"Math. I don't like it much but I have to have it."

Leon stares at him. *Who was this child? The surly teen was gone.* "I didn't sleep well last night. I'm going to lie down for a while." Leon goes to the bedroom.

* * *

I wasn't going to let him off that easy. As he drifts into sleep, I push a dream into his mind. He is back in the electroshock room. The woman he had in there earlier is on the table. He hits the power switch and slowly raises the voltage.

She writhes on the table. Her gag disappears and her ear-splitting shrieks fill the air. Leon puts his hands over his ears, but it isn't enough. One of her hands comes loose from the tiedown and waves in the air. She reaches for him, fingers like claws, flexing.

He slaps at the kill switch, but misses, slaps again. Before he can hit it, she ceases moving. A white cloud rises from her body and swirls around him like a swarm of wasps. He swipes at it wildly, but it closes in. He begins to choke.

With a scream, he sits up in bed. Sweat drips into his eyes. The sheets are twisted in knots and soaked. His breath comes in great gasps. His chest aches. He wraps his arms around himself to keep his pounding heart from bursting out.

"Dad, are you all right?"

Leon looks at the source of the voice. One second, another second, and he recognizes Jon standing in the doorway, a shocked look on his face.

"Bad dream," he rasps out.

"I've had those lately too. They're wicked," said Jon.

"I'll be fine." On shaky legs he goes to the bathroom.

Chapter 20

A message pops up on Leon's tablet as he checks in for work: Report to Section Manager Kwang's office. I feel his twinge of nerves. The receptionist motions for him to proceed directly into the office.

Dr. Yoon and Manager Kwang both rise as he enters.

"Please have a seat, Leon." Yoon gestures to a chair in front of the desk. "How are you feeling today?"

I'm going to push harder to get into Yoon.

Leon shrugs. "I feel fine. I haven't slept well for the last couple of days, and I think it caught up with me yesterday. I'm sorry."

"What's disturbing your sleep?" asked Yoon.

"The death of that subject has been bothering me. I haven't lost one on my table before. When they are no longer able to produce, I call and they are taken away. This one died while I was working on him. I feel like I failed."

Kwang smiles. "Leon, the mistake that resulted in his loss wasn't directly yours. The mistake was leaving him alone with your son before the boy had been trained. That is being rectified."

"Jon is proving quite adept in the medical studies," says Yoon. "He may make a welcome addition to our clinical staff."

I feel Leon relax.

"I'm glad to hear that. I've seen a remarkable change in his attitude at home. He seems to have a direction he lacked before. Thank you for taking him in and giving him a chance."

The iron grip Yoon maintains on his mind is weaker today. I am able to squeeze though the crack, but only slightly. I listen to his mind. He is assessing Leon. Not as to his wellbeing, but as a danger to the Institute. He makes no decision, just gathers facts. He and Kwang will discuss it later.

"Are you okay to go back to work?" asked Kwang, his eyes shifting to Yoon.

"Yes, sir. I was a little shaken up. That's all."

"You shouldn't have been. Let me tell you about the subject you lost." Kwang glanced at papers on his desk. "I cannot give you his name, but he was a convicted serial killer. Though he was found guilty of killing three women, actually two women and a young girl, he admitted to ten other killings."

I feel Leon's shock at this information. My own is greater.

Kwang continues. "In exchange for immunity in the other killings, he provided information and evidence only the killer would have. His burial site provided the bodies. Rather than life in prison without the possibility of parole, he volunteered for our program."

Leon recoils at the thought of who was on his tables. *Would he have volunteered if he knew what would happen in this program?* Leon had no remorse for the man's death, my death. He is sorry he couldn't work on me more.

I flee from Leon's mind, not wanting to hear more of my past.

* * *

In the void, my mind is frozen. Could this be true? Was I everything Kwang had told Leon? I try to search any memory. There is nothing about murders, about a trial, about sentencing. Everything is a blank. The pain I suffered here at the Institute has cauterized my memory.

I wander about, briefly touching other minds, assuring myself of their presence. I do not want to know more about them. The contact is quick, to reassure myself I am here and they are there. I drift in a timelessness that is where I am now.

There is no time in this continuum. I drift and begin to wonder why I feel remorse? Who was I before the torture? That person is not who I became or who I am now. What kind of life did I have that made me into a serial killer? The only way for me to find out is return and find a way into Kwang.

Chapter 21

I am again riding with Leon as he goes to work. His mind is calm. Jon is beside him as they enter. Through Leon, I look at the time stamp as they check in. Two months have passed since Leon's meeting with Kwang. Without my nightmares, they both have done well. Jon goes to the medical lessons, Leon continues to the change room.

He dons the disposable coveralls and passes through the disinfectant room. He walks down the hall with his assistant. It's the hallway I remember. If I had a body, a shiver would pass through me.

A man is in the cell I occupied. What happened to the woman he had before? I don't know but I will find out.

The man struggles against thick straps holding him to the bed. His eyes lock on Leon, who places a mask over his face. Within a few minutes the subject is still. He is placed on the gurney by Leon and his assistant and strapped tightly. They wheel him out. This man is young, in his twenties, I think. His body is fit, muscled, with tattoos. His face is marked by scars, his hair cut close to his scalp.

I recognize the electroshock room as they strap him onto the stainless-steel table, Leon places the electrode pads on his body and sensors to his head, the probe into his anus. As he slides the IV needles into his arms and legs, the man comes to.

"You motherfuckers think you can get anything from me?" he shouts. "I know what this is. I used one like it before. I interrogated hundreds."

Leon attaches the strap that holds his head in place. "I guess you could consider this payback." He puts a gag with electric wires attached into the man's mouth.

The initial charge is low. The man shows no sign of it. Leon increases the voltage. Still, the man remains unmoving. Humming to himself, Leon continues to increase the voltage. The subject closes his eyes as his muscles contract at the current flowing through them. Leon watches the IV lines to assure blood is freely flowing. A light flashes signaling the presence of the chemicals to extract. Leon pushes a button.

I remember that. The electric charges will alternate over his body so that different parts are clenched tightly at any given time. My body never knew where the next shock would be. Behind the gag I hear a moan. Leon increases the voltage. He watches the heartbeat trace on the monitor. The man's body writhes within the restraints.

The alarm from the heart monitor startles Leon. He turns the program off. The subject is still. Leon grabs the defib paddles and smears gel on them. He places them over the heart and steps on the pedal. With a pop, the body convulses. The trace on the monitor is flat. He injects adrenaline into the central line anterior and hits him again. There is a weak flutter. Again, with the paddles. This time the pulse is stronger.

Leon waits for it to even out. When the man's eyes open, Leon says, "Ready for round two?" The man shakes his head as best he can within the restraint. "Prepared or not, here it comes."

I try to contact the man, but only a wall of pain meets me.

I can't stay for this. When this is over, Leon will wash him down, all the residue of torture gone in the only cleaning this man will know.

His pain is my own. I flee from Leon.

Chapter 22

Jon is in the virtual realm again. During the two months I had left him alone,
he had completed the Anatomy sessions and progressed to Diagnosis. This was broken up into different areas of the body and different organs. A body was on the examination table. A list of complaints from the patient was on a chart. Physical data such as blood pressure, pulse rate, oxygenation, respiration, body temperature etc. was on another chart.

Medical history, family history, age, environment at home and work and any genetic information would be factored in. A computer program would match them to give probable causes. Jon had to check those physically on the body. Things such as swelling, infection sites, soreness were factored in.

The computer would then generate a series of tests to be performed. Blood draw, urine sample, throat swabs, biopsies, and others would be recommended. If scans or x-rays were needed, they would be added to the test list.

The focus could be on organs, such as liver, heart, kidneys, skin or brain. Digestion ailments were another focus as were musculature, ligaments, and bones. Each of these areas required intense study and were sub-lessons within the Diagnosis sessions. In the medical world, physicians specialized because of the complicated nature of each. The Artificial Intelligence was all of the specialists combined. Jon needed to learn how to use the AI to diagnose and propose treatments.

What was unique with this program is the computer would take the probable test results before the tests were run and generate an array of causes. These would be assigned probabilities. The program would focus on those and refine the tests to be performed. The easily run and assessed tests were performed as a matter of course. More complicated ones were performed when indicated by other factors.

The If/Then scenarios would generate treatments and medication regimens. These would be checked against the patient data for possible adverse reactions.

All this would happen within minutes. The final result would be a step-by-step procedure. Jon was to perform this analysis and look for what errors could occur. The virtual patient would take the focused tests. Results could lead to further tests.

After the diagnosis, Jon would dissect the virtual patient to see how he had done. This would be repeated many times with different problems. Each was a lesson in itself.

The array of medications available covered the whole spectrum from pharmaceuticals to genetic medications to stem-cell injections. Therapies included both Western and non-traditional. In the virtual world, the patient would follow Jon's program. It included monitoring for possibilities that the patient would not follow the medication regime or therapeutic procedures and the results would pop up.

In cases where surgery was needed, before the first incision, everything possible was known. It would be focused. The Surgery session was next after Diagnosis and Treatment, but that was months away.

In dire cases where the survival was in question, Jon could explain the course of events that were to follow. The patient would decide what to do, including nothing and awaiting the end. The Artificial Intelligence that ran the program made this possible as an advanced tool for doctors. It also kept track of the doctor's performance.

Chapter 23

I am again roaming the void that is my environment. I hadn't noticed groups formed as if drawn by gravity. I reach out with my mind to several souls in one group. They appear to be of the same religion, looking for the afterlife promised to them, yet they are not aware of each other. They seem lost, seeking the Heaven as described by their religion. Some had been told of streets of gold but there is no such thing here. The tale of twenty-seven virgins is particularly bad. Nobody has bodies here.

Somewhere in the religious texts, material reward given by God for good behavior was supposed to happen. Those texts were all written by men. One has to wonder what the total agenda was in writing them. Was it teaching or attracting more followers?

I think about beliefs. Was I religious? I can't remember.

I explore another group, this one quite fundamentalist. Condemning beliefs other than The One is a tool to set them apart and above others. In humans, hatred and bias come easily. One of those souls was a preacher. He has fallen into the trap of pride and status. Judging others comes naturally yet he is lacking in enlightenment and unable to judge himself.

What holds them?

An afterlife of endless torture is more powerful and easier to convey than this place where nothing but minds and souls exist. Fear is a particularly powerful tool to get people to obey.

I see this and more as I drift in this place and observe other souls.

An eternity seeking the things of our past life in a realm where they don't exist and without the bodies to enjoy them is a lie! It is not burning flames that are hell. But that image is easy to picture.

Is it really for an eternity? I don't know. There is no time here. Do souls get another chance to learn the lessons from life? I think they need to acknowledge another chance might work before that could happen. To do so, they would have to recognize the fallacy of material things, of status and pride and judgments–particularly hard in a world as beautiful and tempting as the one we came from.

We are born into an environment of competition and conflict that creates who we are. The ability to see past that is the lesson to be learned.

I drift and find the variety of beliefs has a sameness within a group. There are variations between groups, yet they are similar in basic beliefs. All groups refer to texts as teaching manuals giving them the rules. Yet these groups lose their way and worship the texts and their leaders rather than the lessons. That seems like believing an arithmetic book is mathematics. How does one teach others what I have discovered only after death?

I try to formulate lessons into words and am overwhelmed by the difficulty of that task. It is so much easier to set rules with rewards and punishments for behavior.

Of course, one has to consider who the students are and their abilities. It's like potty training children. Until children become aware of bodily functions, they cannot be potty trained. If people cannot see beyond survival, they haven't the ability to consider more than themselves and the physical world.

I continue drifting. My contact is light, like the touch of a feather. None are aware on my presence. The variety of souls I sense is endless, as are the reasons they remain here.

I realize my quest for revenge against my torturer and my killer is what holds me in this place. I will remain here until I let go. I'm not willing to do that. But I understand what must be done. My quest has expanded beyond Leon and Jon. I now want to stop what is happening. Move up the food chain.

Chapter 24

I ride with Jon to his lesson. Dr. Yoon awaits in his office. It is empty except for a desk and two chairs against one wall. As Jon puts on the headset and enters the virtual reality of the lesson today, I pull back and focus on Yoon. His attention is on Jon and the diagnostic trial for today. His mind is unguarded.

I'm able to slip the tiniest bit of myself into his mind. I know not whether he is capable of sensing me, so I must be cautious. I listen to his thoughts. Unlike Jon or Leon, he concentrates on the lesson. He watches the boy's every move.

I now realize the headset portrays more than the scene of the VR. It monitors eye movements and skin actions. Yoon has done this enough he is able to interpret Jon's intentions before he makes a move. Mentally, the VR notes actions and aims. This is much more than a medical lesson.

Slowly, I ease myself deeper into Yoon. He is very impressed with Jon's ability, but has some doubts about his mental state. An image of Jon walking down his street late at night forms in Yoon's mind.

How did he get that?

They are monitoring him! There must be cameras and microphones in the house also. Kwang and Yoon know of Jon's night restlessness. and his excursions within the neighborhood. I am sure they also know of Leon's problems. Is this standard procedure with all their employees?

Jon finishes his lesson and is released to go home. I stay with Yoon. In Kwang's office, he explains that Jon has a great talent and will be very useful in the medical section.

"What about these nightly excursions?" asks Kwang.

Yoon shrugs. "Thus far, they seem harmless."

"And the restlessness and problems sleeping?"

"He and his father both have problems sleeping. Still, they seem able to cope with the requirements whether at work or in the classroom."

"Has sleeping always been a problem for Leon?"

"We only started monitoring the household after the boy started his lessons. Leon may have had trouble before, but as I say, his work has been exemplary. He shows no signs of deterioration."

"He did mention that the unexpected loss of the subject he was working on bothered him. Could this have started then?"

I sense Yoon thinking this over.

"When the woman he was working on became exhausted and spent, he did not hesitate to turn her over to the disposal service. I did not see any problems then."

"The difference, of course, is that his son was involved in the loss of the man."

I tried to get more sense of Kwang. His mind was like a fortress. It would take time to break into that. Still, there was a slight crack.

"Yes, that is true," answered Yoon. "During the interview, my impression was that the boy and his father were not close, yet the boy sought his father's approval. His acceptance here at the Institute has changed that dynamic somewhat. Jon has found something that is challenging and he enjoys. He is quite bright, more so than the father."

A thoughtful look crosses Kwang's face. "Do you see that as a problem?"

"Leon struggles with the lessons Jon breezes through. It isn't a problem yet, but may become so in the future. I'm sure there exists some jealously in the father. If we want to push Jon ahead, perhaps he should move him into the dormitory."

"Let's think on that for a while. In the meantime, maintain the surveillance."

As Yoon leaves, I sense darkness arising within him. It is directed toward Leon.

Chapter 25

I am with Jon as he lies awake in his bed. It is Saturday night, and music drifts into his open window. Somebody is having a party he isn't part of, and it rankles, though he wouldn't go if invited. He harbors resentment that others can have fun while he cannot. He hasn't explored himself enough to understand the problem is with him.

It is late, near midnight, when he rises, dresses in his dark clothes, and slips out of the house. The music has died, but the lights in the girl's bedroom, her house at the end of his street blaze. She is having a party, maybe a sleepover. He slips from house to house until he is crouched against the wall below her open window.

Voices, girl's voices, and laughter trickle out. Cautiously, he stands and peeks in. A slight breeze ruffles the curtains giving him occasional glimpses inside. Four girls in pajamas are in the room. Two are lying on the bed, two more sit on the floor. They talk about boys in school and other girls. The chatter is interrupted occasionally with peals of laughter. He listens, enjoying his participation from afar. He feels an ache of longing to be part of a group like that, friends he can talk with. AND girls! He squats below the window until his legs ache. The voices begin to quiet as the conversation dies down. He stands for a last look. One of the girls comes to the window to close it.

She sees him and screams. He spins away and runs as if pursued by a demon. Glancing behind him, he sees the lights come on in other rooms of the house.

Shit! Shit! Shit! A dog barks.

He looks back at the house. The silhouette of a man is in the doorway. He continues running past his house to the end of the block. After turning the corner, he ducks into the alley. Scaling the fence into his yard, he tries to quiet his breathing. Still gasping, he slips into his house. He leans against the back door as if to prevent it from opening. He listens. His house is quiet, but the dog still barks outside. His heart still pounds. Back in bed, he chuckles. *That was close.* Getting caught will probably ruin his chances at the Institute.

* * *

I feel Jon's excitement. He had been scared, panicked even, but now he enjoys the thrill. I project one of the bodies from his lessons into his mind. It's one without skin, bare muscles and sinews. It turns its head, eyeless sockets seemingly to stare, and beckons for him to come closer.

He screams as he leaps from the bed. His heart throbs and he sucks in air. His door opens.

"Jon, are you all right?" asked his father, as he steps toward the boy.

"Bad dream, Dad. I'm okay."

"I know what those are, though I haven't had one in a few weeks."

"Yeah, this is my first in a while."

Leon sits on the bed. "You want to talk about it?"

"I was in the virtual reality session and one of the bodies moved."

Leon is quiet for a minute. "That happened to me a few days ago."

"You were awake? "

"It was during one of my lessons."

"That would be creepy!"

"It was. I had to cut the lesson short."

"Dad, I don't remember having nightmares until a few months ago."

"Same with me. At first, they involved the subject who died on my table."

"That's what mine were too! What's going on?"

"I don't know, son, but we can't let anyone at the Institute know."

* * *

If I had a body, I'd be laughing my ass off. Perhaps I need to inject different images.

Chapter 26

Dr. Yoon and Dr. Kwang watch the drone video of Jon's last nightly excursion.

"If he gets caught, we could be in danger," says Yoon.

"What do you suggest?" asks Kwang.

"He has shown to be uniquely talented in the medical area. It is possible he could be trained to operate our remote clinics. I would hate to lose the opportunity to at least try. Perhaps we can bring him into one of the dorm rooms and let him stay here."

"We have another candidate staying here, don't we?"

"Yes, sir. She was smuggled across the Mexican border as part of a human trafficking operation. She managed to escape and turned up at a mission in shock. One of our medical assistants alerted us. The shelter was overcrowded and we were able to make arrangements for her to stay here. We started schooling her, and like Jon, she is quite intelligent. Her aptitude in the medical area is remarkable."

"What about her parents? Surely they are looking for her."

"When the cartel took over her village, many were killed or fled. Her parents were murdered in front of her. Even if she is returned to Mexico, she has nowhere to go. Elena has chosen to remain with us."

Kwang shook his head. "Sad story."

"Yes, but with a good ending so far."

"Will Leon and his wife let Jon live with us?"

Yoon smiled. "If we show Leon this video and explain the threat, he has no choice."

"Do it. Move him here tomorrow."

"What about Leon? Is he all right?"

"His performance has been slipping since that subject died on his table. Our bugs at this house picked up bickering with his wife, and there are liquor bottles in his trash."

"Leave the monitors at the house. We'll have to watch for any additional problems."

"I'll program in the actions we want the AI to flag."

* * *

Leon patiently explained to his wife for the third time Jon would be living at the Institute during his training. "It's a great opportunity for him. He has an aptitude for the medical field, might even become a doctor."

Barbara snorted. "That boy a doctor! I pity anybody sick enough to see him."

"I know you'll miss him, but it is the best for him."

"Hah! I won't miss him. Let them take care of his bedwetting and roaming around at night."

"You knew about his walks?"

"Unlike you, I do not sleep like the dead. Or have nightmares. Sure, I knew."

"Why didn't you tell me?"

"And what would you have done? Telling him to stop wouldn't work, like wetting the bed. What do you care if he lives at the Institute? It's one less mouth to feed, one less worry."

"But he's our son."

"They'll be better parents at the Institute than we've been. He'll be fine. Maybe now we can take that vacation you've wanted. I'd like to get away for a while."

* * *

Chapter 27

I sense the turmoil within Leon. Having the boy gone was a relief but also a sense of failure. He'd tried to make up for the years of neglect this last three months, but he knew it was too little, too late.

Guilt was building. In addition to the remorse over the boy, the box in which he isolated his feeling about his job had cracked open. Images of the man dying kept haunting him. He was not successful at putting the new subjects into that box either.

Thanks to me. I will not let that stop.
I'm willing to let Jon alone–for a while.

* * *

Another message of a meeting with his manager, Kwang, pops up as Leon checks in.

I am not sure what this is about, but it will give me another opportunity to work my way into the psyches of Yoon and Kwang. I feel Leon's trepidation as he enters Kwang's office.

Kwang gestures toward the chair in front of his desk. "Have a seat, Leon. We appreciate your decision to have Jon stay with us. We think it would be the best for the boy."

I sense bitterness in Leon. I reach out toward Kwang. His mind is unguarded. I move in. He is so smug in the security of his position. This man is Mr. Control.

"I understand you have been going through some mental crisis lately. Your work has suffered."

"I'll do better, Dr. Kwang," Leon said." Now that I know Jon is well taken care of, I can focus better."

"That is good," said Yoon. "We would like for you to reduce your intake of alcohol also. It clouds your mind."

Leon freezes.

I feel the shock go through him from their knowledge of his drinking. He only does that to quell the dreams and images haunting him, he tells himself. A question arises. How do they know about that?

"We monitor all of our employees," said Kwang, as if he reads Leon's mind. "You can imagine the controversy public knowledge of our Extraction program would raise."

I feel both Kwang and Yoon study Leon for his reaction.

"Yes, sir. It could be quite a problem. You don't have to worry about me. I'm fine.

"That's good to know, Leon," said Kwang.

"To address your sleep problem, we would like to start you on some medication." Yoon hands Leon a bottle of pills. "These are a mild sleep aid. I am sure after a week, you will be well rested and won't need them anymore. Take one each night before bed in the meantime."

"Thank you, sir. When can I see Jon?"

"Would you like to have lunch with him today?" asks Kwang. "He eats at noon."

"We'll have somebody come get you," says Yoon.

Leon looks from one to the other for a second, but senses the meeting is over.

* * *

Being inside two minds as both people talk is a new experience. I know what they are going to say before they speak.

"We'll watch him carefully," says Yoon. "At the first sign of continued breakdown we'll have to take action."

An image of Leon and his wife's bodies floats in Yoon's mind. It is the same in Kwang's.

* * *

Leon has never been in the dining room at the Institute. It is a cafeteria with twelve four-by tables. Jon and Leon carry their trays to an empty table.

"This is nice," says Leon looking around.

"Yeah, and the food is good," answers Jon, He'd opted for the tuna sandwich and chips with a small salad. Leon had gotten the enchiladas with rice and beans. He hadn't had Mexican food in a long time.

"How are your lessons going?" asked Leon.

I feel his disappointment at having to drop his own lessons while he overcomes his problems.

"Great, Dad. The Diagnostics and Treatment session is much harder than the Anatomy session. The AI really helps, but there's still a lot of judgement and trial to get the right regimen."

Regimen is a word Leon never heard his son use before. He likes Jon's greater vocabulary and maybe advancement?

"How is your room?"

"It's good. I have my own work station tied into the system. I can take lessons whenever I want, even in the middle of the night if I can't sleep. That doesn't happen very much."

Better than roaming the streets, thinks Leon.

"Dr. Yoon says I'm doing well. My scores are seventy five percent."

"Your mom will be glad to hear that. She misses you," Leon lied. "Have you had any more dreams?"

"Not since I got here.," Jon says around a mouthful of sandwich.

"Are you the only student?"

"There are a few others. We haven't really talked much. They're older than me. I think they go to the university and come here for a few sessions." Jon takes a huge bite of his sandwich.

Leon watches him chew.

"They don't live here, except for Elena. She's about as old as me. We eat together sometimes. She doesn't talk much." Jon stuffs more chips in his mouth.

"You shouldn't eat so fast," admonishes Leon.

"We don't get a lot of time for lunch," cramming the last of his sandwich in his mouth. "Gotta go, Dad. Maybe we can do this again soon." With that, Jon strode out the door.

Leon glanced down at this plate. He'd hardly touched his enchiladas. His appetite was gone.

Chapter 28

I'm with Leon as he watches the tough guy stripped naked and shackled to the chair in the freezer. His lips are blue, frost has built up around his nose and mouth. He shivers within his bindings. The freezer is cold enough to lower the body core temperature over time, but not cause extensive frostbite. He passes out.

Leon enters, attaches the sensors and inserts the IVs. He inserts a gag in the man's mouth.

I know what is ahead and I'm glad I have no body.

He rolls the chair out, makes the connections to the monitors, tightens the restraints and does a last-minute check. A hoist picks up the chair and man. They are positioned over a vat of warm water. Leon turns on the pump to remove blood and fluids from the man through the IV. He is plunged in.

Through Leon, I watch as his subject's eyes fly open, his throat convulses as he tries to scream through the gag. His eyes bulge and his face is red. He thrashes as much as the restraints will allow. The heart monitor shows two hundred forty BPM. He passes out.

Leon brings the chair out of the vat, lowers it to the floor, turns off the IV pump and disconnects the sensors. The only sound is the dripping of water and the man's raspy breathing.

This pain I remember.

Leon steps out for a smoke while the subject warms and his vitals return to normal. He'd kicked the habit years ago, but lately started again due to the stress. That's what he tells himself.

I have only been in this small patio when I'm with Leon.

He sits on the concrete bench. Two sails give the only shade and color to the otherwise concrete walls and slab floor. He lights his cigarette and exhales in a long stream.

His thoughts drift to his son. He should be relieved that Jon is doing well in the training program, but a bit of jealously creeps in. He closes his eyes and sighs.

In his mind, he is back in the virtual reality of his anatomy lesson. The image of the skeleton arm thrashing about while he tries to attach the wrist appears. He flinches as the empty eye sockets seem to stare at him and the jaw hinges open and shut. Why is this happening to him?

He wishes he had a drink. *Not now. They are watching me.* Stubbing out his cigarette, he rises and returns to his subject. This man had been an interrogator, a torturer for the military. That was evident. Leon also understands he enjoyed inflicting pain on those he questioned. Sometimes those sessions continued long after the last bit of information had been given up. A touch of pleasure rose in Leon at being able to give back. He wanted to know nothing more.

The man's face reflects his resignation to his plight. "What do you want to know? I'll tell you everything."

Leon says nothing as he wheels him back into the freezer.

The scream echoes within the room. "What do you want?"

Leon remains mute, his face expressionless, as he closes the door.

Chapter 29

I have decided there is no life after death.

However, there is consciousness. I say this because the definition of life, a physical thing that grows and replicates doesn't apply to a non-physical existence. So, is there consciousness after life?

I am here.

Does consciousness come from life or life from consciousness? Since I am here, at least the first of those questions is true. Did that part of me exist before the life I left?

I now believe this exists on another plane from life and I'm on that plane along with all these other souls. I also see that plane extending over that state of existence we call life like the sky over the Earth.

It is endless and timeless. To me, that answers the second question.

That then begs the question: Is my consciousness unique to me? If it is, then it existed before my latest life and may exist again in another. If it is not true, then that part of me is a fragment of something much greater. These are musings as I roam this plane, this dimension. If I am part of something much greater, can I expand my awareness until I can fathom this? I try.

I feel my awareness growing and more of the plane becomes apparent. It is endless. I try to contact other souls as I expand.

Suddenly, I am stopped. What does this mean? Try as I might, I can go no farther. There is nothing physical in this existence, so it's not a wall, but a block to my exploration. I hang motionless but then feel the pull of my link to my torturer. Is that what keeps me from moving on? I sense it is more. What could be beyond? Something to think about.

* * *

I haven't been with Jon for a while. Perhaps it is time for a visit. He is in the dining room, sitting with a girl. Neither of them speaks until Jon asks Elena, that's her name, about her training. She's been at the Institute longer than Jon and is more advanced. She describes the Surgery Program.

"At first the lessons were easy, but after cardiology, I'll move to the brain."

"That sounds hard," said Jon.

"The assessment precedes any surgery. Many times, things can be done with only an insertion cut. Tools can be fed into the veins for say a valve replacement. No need to open anyone up."

"The teacher instructs you about those?"

"Yes. With the Artificial Intelligence assisting, it is quite easy. I mostly oversee. For surgery, it will present the whole procedure. If I approve, it will move ahead."

"You don't do any hands-on?"

"Actually, my hands are in gloves that are moved by the AI. I learn the feel from the machine. It will highlight danger areas and cautions. The movement of the gloves diminishes as the lessons continue until it is my hands doing the surgery."

"Wow! That sounds complicated."

"At first, I made some fatal mistakes but my skill level improved."

"What's next?"

"Cardiology is straightforward. Operable cancer is difficult. The degree is not easily detected. Many times, the extent is unknown until after the surgery starts. I'm looking forward to those lessons."

"You want to be a surgeon?"

"Yes. What about you?"

Jon smiled. "I like the Diagnostics and Treatment lessons. I seem to have a feel for it. It's like I'm inside the patient. I can move to the site of the problem and follow the cause back and see how to treat it."

"So, unlike western medicine, you treat the cause and not the symptom?"

"It's what I'm learning to do. Many times, the cause is environmental, like diet or an allergy."

* * *

Leon arrives home after a particularly bad day. Something went wrong with the tough guy he was treating. He's still alive, but his heartbeat is irregular, his breathing shallow. The session is cut short. He will check on him tomorrow, but a resumption may have to wait until he becomes more normal.

Leon is worried. The cold stare from Dr. Yoon when he reported the issue was unnerving. He could see disapproval in the doctor's eyes. Leon knows this wasn't his fault. He did everything correctly. After the first electroshock session, the man had gone into cardiac arrest. Leon used the defib paddles to bring him back, but he wasn't normal. His heartbeat was weak and erratic, his breathing shallow. Leon put an oxygen mask on him and waited. After an hour, he was still unconscious, nothing changed. He had the man taken back to his cell.

The first whiskey helps calm Leon's nerves. The second slows his mind. He sits at the kitchen table staring at the television. It's turned off, the screen is black. After the third whiskey, he goes to the bedroom and flops onto the bed fully dressed.

I bring the image of Yoon's face into Leon's mind. He stirs but doesn't waken. I follow that with an image of the last session with the subject strapped to the table, electrodes taped to him, IVs taking blood from him and monitors beeping that he has flatlined.

Leon groans as he watches himself working to revive the man. The heart monitor shows erratic blips. I force words into his mind: *Not again! Please not again!* He rolls to one side of the bed, leans over, and vomits.

Chapter 30

I'm with Leon in Kwang's office. The manager motions him to a chair next to Dr. Yoon. Thank God he had the weekend to recover from the drunken stupor he'd been in Friday, Leon thinks. His head still hurt, but not the throbbing pain of Saturday morning.

"From the video, you had a problem with the latest subject. Is he recovered?" asked Kwang.

"Yes, sir. When I checked in on him this morning, he seemed fine."

"What happened?" asked Yoon.

"I'm not sure. I followed our normal procedure and monitored his vitals." Leon glanced at Yoon. "But he didn't recover from the shock treatment. His heart stopped. I began the recovery process. He came back, but his pulse was irregular and his breathing shallow. I waited for him to recover, but he wasn't fully conscious so I terminated the session."

"It sounds to me like this subject had problems we didn't detect in the initial screening," said Yoon. He turned to Kwang. "Perhaps it is best if we leave him alone for a few days."

"Good idea," said Kwang. "In the meantime, Leon, we think you should take some time off, maybe take the wife on a little vacation."

I move into Kwang. This might be a vacation Leon wouldn't return from. He and Yoon haven't decided yet whether Leon is stable, not a threat.

I feel Leon flinch. He has the same thought. He is fighting to keep his face impassive. "Sir, I really am fine."

Kwang raises his hand. "We know that, but you haven't taken any time off in quite a while. Take a week. Go enjoy yourself."

Thank you, sir. I will.

I feel the turmoil in Leon's mind as he returns to the locker room.

He removes some of his personal items, picks up the athletic bag and puts them in it. He has to consider what this vacation was about.

At home, he announces to his wife they will be taking a break. The look on her face shows surprise. Leon gives her a hug and whispers "Bugs in the house. They are watching. Show no reaction."

"Are we going somewhere?" asks Barbara.

"I think we'll get out of town for a week or so," answers Leon. "We'll figure out where once we're on the road."

"What about Jon?"

"I spent some time with him. He's doing well at the Institute, won't miss us for a few days. How about a sandwich? I haven't eaten since breakfast."

Through Leon's eyes, I watch his wife bustle around the kitchen making a tuna sandwich. Leon glances around the room looking for any obvious cameras. He sees none.

"Pack a few things. I never saw the Grand Canyon. Let's take a tour." He takes a large bite from the sandwich. It tastes like cardboard.

* * *

I enter Kwang.

He and Yoon watch Leon and his wife hastily pack things and go to the car. The cameras in the house give them full surveillance.

"Are you worried?" asked Kwang.

"They had things ready. He suspects."

"Let's have our asset tail them. At the first hint of a problem, they'll have an accident. I hate to lose him." Kwang shook his head. "He's proven quite good at the extractions."

"We can't take a chance."

"No problems with the boy?"

"I've been with him since he started his classes. He doesn't seem to miss time with his parents. They weren't close. Still, we'll watch him also."

"Any recurrence of his night walking episodes?"

"He's so wrapped up in the classes, nothing else has come up." Yoon has his hand on his chin in thought. "Though he has been sharing his meals with Elena."

"That could be a good thing."

"I think so too."

Chapter 31

I was in Leon as he casually pulled away from their house. His time in military intelligence made him very wary. He puts his finger to his lips again to signal his wife not to talk. He is sure the car is bugged and has a tracker. It's what he'd do.

He glances at Barbara. "We haven't taken time off in so long, this will be welcome. I need to get some gas."

At the gas station, he performs a quick search for any tracking devices and bugs inside. He finds both. He places them on the seat between he and his wife.

When she gets in the car, he points at the devices. "Let's take the scenic route. Did you get any road food?"

Barbara holds up a bag of Cheetos and a large Icee.

"Perfect." He gets back on the road and turns the radio to a talk station.

* * *

I have no doubt Kwang and Yoon believe Leon is a threat and will kill him–perhaps is wife also. Sending them on a vacation means the crime will happen far away from the Institute. A feeling of satisfaction rises within me. But it doesn't last. Setting them up to be murdered in a world I no longer inhabit seems wrong. This drive for revenge—yes, I acknowledge that's what it is— does nothing for me. I'm not there to gloat over my actions. In my past life before I was a prisoner, maybe that would be all right. Maybe. I still don't know what I was before.

Being able to get inside Leon's head is having an effect on me. I had the blind drive for revenge because the pain he caused is all I remember of him. Now I see he didn't enjoy what he was doing. It was a job. He had walled off the emotions and performed the torture like a machine.

I would imagine a soldier in war would have to do the same thing or develop an intense hatred for the enemy. I can see where an illusion that the enemy is purely evil would wear thin and become the seed for Post Traumatic Stress Disorder. Leon is not purely evil.

I travel back into my new world. I withdraw into myself creating a shell around me. This is the opposite of what I did before, expanding and reaching out. It is like a womb. Here, I can examine myself. My obsession with Leon keeps me tied to my life before I died. The desire to let that go is growing stronger. I study my feelings about saving him.

To do his job, he isolated himself from humanity. Does he deserve to die for that? I died and here I am. He would be here also. The thought stops me.

Even if I want to save him, can I? My tie to Kwang and Yoon is not strong and having Leon or Jon present helps. I need more sessions with them to strengthen it. Leon's gone, so it must be Jon.

* * *

Jon is in a virtual reality session with a subject. She is talking to him about problems she is having. Jon listens, keeping notes on his tablet. He steps close to examine her. The AI is indicating a problem with her gallbladder. He puts his hands on her. *I put images in his head.*

She screams and reaches for him, fingers clawing. He steps back. She levitates from the table and flies toward him. Jon screams and rips the headset off. The room is empty except for Dr. Yoon.

"What's wrong?"

"She tried to hurt me."

"What! That's not possible."

"She did."

"Let's watch the replay," says Yoon. They both watch the large monitor on the wall as Yoon directs it to just played the session. The woman is on the examining table. Jon asks her question and she tells him of pain. Jon approaches her and puts his hands on her abdomen. Suddenly, he jumps back his hands thrust forward as if warding off an attack.

She remains on the table. He grasps the headset and tears it off.

Jon stares from the monitor to the doctor. "I don't understand,"

"Perhaps you need a break. The studying has been nonstop. Go back to your room, maybe lie down for a while."

Jon nods. He doesn't want a break. This is like the dreams he was having before.

While Jon is with Yoon, I strengthen my link into the Dr. He is worried about his star pupil. After Jon is gone, he replays the video. Whatever happened with Jon was within his head. He plays it again. I don't know if I can do it, but I push an image of the woman floating above the table into his mind. He sees something but no more than a hint, a flash of a white shadow rising. It's brief, then gone. He sits back and shakes his head.

He runs it again. I repeat pushing the image. The result is the same, but the shadow is more solid. I am learning. He runs it again, but this time he plays it frame-by-frame. I do nothing. He repeats it at normal speed. The white shadow reappears.

Twice more he repeats the sequence at slow speed and at normal. He calls IT and tells them to run a diagnostic on the software. Thirty minutes later he is assured the software is fine.

He runs the sequence again. *This time I do nothing. I'm in his head.*

Chapter 32

I'm with Leon as he drives to Albuquerque and drops his wife off to meet her sister. There is no record of her sister in the Institute files. He stays only long enough to carry her bags into the convenience store and departs for Arizona. He knows they are tracking him and hopes the stop looks like a short rest. He turns the radio on as he passes the Walking Sands rest stop and sings along with the country western music.

Six more hours to Sierra Vista. He'll stop in Hatch and eat at Sparkey's, the best green chili burgers in the country. In Deming he'll gas up for the rest of the trip. He'd be in Sierra Vista for breakfast.

The roads are straight and this time the traffic is light. He's exhausted from work and stress.

Coming out of Lordsburg, he starts to drift off. The car heads for the shoulder.

I put an image of myself screaming around the gag at the electroshock. He jerks awake in time to keep from going off the road.

Why did I do that? I could have had my revenge at his own hand. It would solve the problem with the Institute at the same time.

I don't want to solve their problem. I want to create more.

Every time Leon gets sleepy, I place images from work in his head. He stays awake. As the sun is coming up, he passes Benson and takes the exit from I-10 to Sierra Vista. An hour later, he falls into bed at the Super 8 motel. I let him sleep.

* * *

Jon reads for a while, but he can't concentrate. If his dreams come back, what will he do? He can't go outside for a walk here. In fact, he hasn't been outside since he moved in. Would they even let him out? He wonders what the girl at the end of the street is doing.

At dinner, he sits with Elena.

"Jon are you all right? You seem distracted."

"I had some trouble in the last session. Something with the software, I think."

"I had that soon after I started here. They said they'd solved it."

"Have you been outside since you arrived?"

"Oh sure. They've taken me on several excursions. In the winter, we went to one of the ski areas. It was really neat. Cold too. Been shopping in Denver several times. They gave me money to buy whatever I wanted."

"Someone was with you the whole time?"

"Sure. I can't drive and don't know my way around. Yoon and I went to a movie and afterward a really nice restaurant."

"But you haven't just walked around this area?"

"No, but I really don't want to. Do you?"

"My parents' house isn't far, so I've walked around here before."

"Ask Dr. Yoon. I'm sure he won't have a problem."

* * *

Jon taps on Yoon's office door.

"Come in," says the doctor. "Hi, Jon. Your next session isn't until tomorrow. What can I do for you?"

"Sir, I'd like to go outside for a walk around the neighborhood, maybe visit my mother."

Yoon stares at him for a few seconds. "Certainly, you can go outside. I'll arrange for someone to go with you. I do need to tell you that your parents took a vacation. They should be back in a couple of weeks."

I feel Jon start at the news.

"Dad didn't say anything about a vacation."

"We had a break in the schedule yesterday and I offered him the days off. He took it. I don't know if they're home or went on a little trip." Yoon lied.

"Oh," said Jon. "I'd still like to walk around. There are some things at the house I'd like to get."

"I'll have one of our assistants go with you. Though the neighborhood is usually safe, we're responsible for you. When do you want to go?"

"Is today too soon?"

Yoon smiled. "Not at all. Let me make a call." He picked up his phone, punched in a number. "Alex, Jon would like to take a walk. Would you go with him?" He listened. "I'll have him meet you at the front lobby in thirty minutes. Thank you."

"There you are, Jon. Have a good walk."

Chapter 33

I need to learn more about this place I'm in. As I have no eyes or ears or body, the only way I can feel anything here is with my mind. I reached out to some other minds before, and I can sense there are more. I expand my senses, not in the focused manor as before, but widely, trying to take in as much as possible. The others here are as dense as a mountain fog, each particle another mind.

I change my spectrum of senses like changing the color of a light beam. Each of the particles has a connection to its past life. Some are focused on individuals, like mine. Others link to a place, while more focus on objects. All of them have these links. The lines of connection are like a spider's web surrounding their past lives.

Do the minds of the dead surround and infiltrate the world of the living? I study this. These minds are on another plane. Only a few are able to interject themselves into the three-dimensional world. Why am I able to do this?

I enter several other souls. Only a few are linked to a place that holds a strong connection to their past lives. I find others linked to objects, another linked to a person, like I am. I'm beginning to understand. For the links of the dead to affect that world requires living people whose minds are receptive and can be entered. Without a sensitive person, there is no change. If a tree falls in the forest with no one around, does it make a sound? Who knows?

Here's what I've learned: The links of the dead surround the world of the living. Surround is the only term I can think of but it is more of an infusion, like air upon the Earth, but on another plane. Only when a strong link exists and a sensitive person is present can those links allow me to sense the world of the living. Those links can be with other people, objects, or places, but the only sensitive are aware.

I'm able to enter other spirits without them knowing. Are others entering me?

Chapter 34

Leon woke to sunlight streaming through a crack in the drapes covering the window. He glanced at the clock beside the bed. It was noon, time to get up. He needed to find a place to live and work. And he needed transportation. He'd removed the tracker and put it on a semi at the truck stop. They'd figure that out and start backtracking. He needed to get rid of the car. First things first.

After cleaning up, he went down for the complimentary breakfast. It was the usual buffet. Next stop was the bank. He opened an account under his false identity, Robert Larson. The eight-thousand-dollar deposit wouldn't raise any red flags and it would give him a credit card. He drove to Bisbee, then Naco, Mexico. There, he sold the car, walked across the border and had a taxi take him to the bus depot in Bisbee.

The bus dropped him at the depot in Sierra Vista. Another taxi took him to a used car dealer where he bought an old Toyota. It had 85,000 miles, but for a Toyota it was just getting broken in.

Time to find a place to live. Close to Ft. Huachuca, he found an apartment. Basic with a lot of GIs living in the complex. They'd move in and out depending on their next assignment. The furnishings were old, the AC unit groaned, and his neighbors liked to party.

He went online and ended up with a job as a short-haul trucker for a furniture company moving stock from its Tucson warehouse. He was set for a while. As he packed his things in the motel, he knew he needed to figure out how to contact Jon and his wife without the Institute finding out.

* * *

Jon and Alex took the bus to Jon's neighborhood. They got off and walked the two blocks to the house. Jon tried the door, but it was locked, a sure sign nobody was home. Jon pulled out his key and they entered.

"Hello. Anybody here?" called Jon. No answer. Alex followed Jon as he checked out the house. It was neat, but things one would normally take on a vacation were gone–toothbrushes, clothes, water bottles. In the closet, he saw the go-bags were gone.

"Alex, I'm going to get the mail. Have a seat. I'll be right back." At the mailbox, he quickly went through the mail. Bills, ads, no letters. He went back inside. He stacked the mail in a box.

"I'm going to have to pay some bills while Mom and Dad are gone. Dad set me up on the household account." Alex nodded. He sat at the breakfast table and wrote a couple of checks, put return address stickers on them and stamps.

"I need to get some clothes." In the bedroom, he put underwear, pants and shirts in a gym bag. In a Ziplok he put toothpaste, toothbrush, comb, and deodorant. In a side pocket he put an envelope some note paper and a pen. He set the bag in the living room. "Alex, I'm going to walk around the neighborhood for a few minutes. Come if you want."

They walked to the cul-de-sac and back, then to the small park a block away. Kids were flying kites.

"You ever flown a kite, Alex?"

"Nah."

"I have a couple back at the house. Maybe when we come back we can take a little time. It's really relaxing."

"Yeah, sure. Look, we should probably be getting back pretty soon."

"I know. I have another session in an hour."

At the house, Jon got his bag and they set out for the bus stop.

* * *

I follow both Jon and Leon. I know what's going on with them. When Jon puts the pen and paper in his bag, I pick up on his idea of how to contact his parents. I can help, but why am I considering this? Something inside me doesn't like the idea of them being set up, especially by the

Institute. I leave Leon and Jon alone and focus on Kwang and Yoon.

* * *

I can enter them but not influence them…yet. I'll keep working on it. Kwang is with Yoon in the VR room. They are watching Jon go through his session.

"The boy has quite a talent for diagnosing," said Yoon. "The virtual subject I've chosen today has a small tumor on the pancreas. Her symptoms are slight, her pain minimal, but she senses something is not right. Untreated, the tumor will lead to cancer." He glances at Jon who's standing a few feet away. "He's wearing earbuds and can't hear us. The monitor shows the VR examination room. Let's watch."

I go into Jon in the virtual reality lesson.

The test subject is on an examining table. "Tell me where the pain is," says Jon.

"It's not bad, but it's in my stomach and spreads to my back.

"What else?"

"I don't feel like eating, I've lost some weight. And I itch a lot."

"No insect bites or anything?"

"No."

Jon walks over to her. He holds his hands an inch above her abdomen, not touching her. He moves them above her body slowly, his eyes closed.

"I recommend a scan to check you out."

He writes in his tablet: Potential pancreatic tumor. Might be early stage of cancer. Treatable now with surgery.

Kwang nods. "He nailed that one. If that were a real patient, who would perform the surgery?"

"Our robot surgeons would do the work, overseen by me, the certified doctor, and Elena."

"The robots are up to the task?"

"They will be soon. It could be done arthroscopically. We could do it in the clinic with her as an outpatient."

"We will need rooms for recovery."

"We plan to use chambers for that at first. The chambers are like a large VR headset giving the illusion of being in a room. When the patients are able to take care of themselves they'll be moved to a room."

"Let's watch Jon again. The next patient won't be so easy." They both watch as another virtual appears on the examining table.

"Why are you here?" asks Jon.

"I have these itchy spots on my back and shoulders. They won't go away."

Jon looks at several of the spots. "What have you put on them?"

"First I used some moisturizing creams. Nothing happened. I tried Benadryl, but again nothing changed. Lately, I've tried some across the counter cortisone. It helped some. They got smaller but wouldn't go away. I'm afraid they might be skin cancer."

"They're not skin cancer." Jon moves his hands above the man. He sits on a stool and thinks for a few minutes. "You have an autoimmune condition called discoid lupus. It's a relatively mild form of lupus that normally doesn't become the systemic form."

"What do I have to do?"

"I'm going to refer you to one of our treatment specialists." He picks up his tablet and wrote: recommend a quinine-based medication. This will require periodic eye tests as one side effect is loss of vision field. In many instances, the discoid lupus will burn itself out after a while and disappear." He logs in his notes.

"He got it," said Dr. Yoon. "That is an amazing diagnosis that usually requires months of testing including biopsies and of course lab work. You see what I mean about him?"

"When does he see a real patient?"

"Tomorrow. We've brought in someone from the Free Clinic. You want to observe?"

"Yes. What is his next area of study?" asked Kwang.

"Normally we would take a student into the Surgery program, but I think he'd be much more valuable in our new clinic if we intensified his diagnostic training. The amount of testing and lab work eliminated would be a huge cost savings."

"How are the plans for the clinic going?"

"We will continue to offer training classes in conjunction with the University medical school. They have already seen the benefit of our system. Those students offer us a chance to find talent. We're always looking for the right personnel to staff the clinic. We'll need another certified doctor in addition to myself and registered nurses on board to get the proper licenses. The real work will be done by our students, our robot surgeons, and our AI system. We'll self-insure."

"And our patients?"

"We will operate on a self-pay basis. No insurance or Medicare. That might sound like we'll only be able to take high-end patients who can afford to pay. Not so. Under this system, costs will be within the reach of even the poor. We will offer financing or trade for services."

"The AMA and regulating boards will go along?"

"We'll start as a free clinic serving those who can't pay. I expect we will have lawsuits and charges filed, but we will stay within the law. Gratis services are much harder to sue. For the first few years, our major expenses will probably be lawyers. This clinic will pave the way for a new medical system, one of the future. It will be practically automated. Personnel like Jon and Elena will be paid well, but most of our overhead will be equipment upkeep and utilities. The medications we're developing will be used as *supplements* not drugs.

Kwang nodded. "As you know, we own this building. You make it sound simple, but I suspect the devil is in the details."

* * *

I am stunned by this revelation.

My original thoughts were that the Institute was a pharmaceutical company ready to develop new drugs They would charge exorbitant fees, rape the public, the insurance companies and the government. It appears to not be the case. The Institute will be walking a fine line. The system will not stand for anything outside of traditional medicine. Especially if it's successful.

Chapter 35

I'm in Jon for his first live session.

Jon looks at the live man on the examining table. They're in a part of the Institute he hasn't visited before, a clinic. I can feel his nervousness.

The man stares at Jon. "Aren't you a little young to be a doctor?"

"I'm not a doctor. I do diagnostics. What problems are you having?"

The man frowns. "I got stomach problems, pains and cramping especially when I gotta take a crap. Sometimes it's so bad I break out in a sweat."

"Are you in pain right now?"

The man nods. Jon walks over to the table. He holds his hands over the man. "Close your eyes." Something passes through me and enters Jon. He sees the man as a body of energies flowing in a system. We enter him. Jon feels the man's pain and winces. I feel it too. We travel through his stomach, into the intestinal track and through the colon. I don't know what Jon's seeing, but he has found a disruption in the energy flow.

We're back inside Jon's body.

Jon taps on his tablet. He looks up. "You've got diverticulitis."

"What's that?"

"Inside your intestines these little cups rise up. They trap food bits and get irritated causing pain and cramping. If you ignore the pain, it can get serious and puncture the walls of your colon. That's a big problem."

"I can't ignore that pain. What do I have to do?"

"I'm going to refer you to one of our treatment specialists."

Jon talks to the patient as he enters his notes on his tablet: "First, I recommend an antispasmodic to calm things down. Take it only as needed. It should relieve some of the discomfort until things are straightened out. Then a diet change. No foods with little seeds like blackberries. Caution with spicy foods that can cause irritation. No popcorn or alcohol. After your colon is cleaned out, stick to a diet of fruits and vegetables with fiber supplements every day. Drink fruit juices. Restrict processed foods. It's important to improve elimination. With favorable results, you may not need further treatment."

"I'm kinda living on the street at times. I eat whatever I can.

"Be more selective in your dumpster diving. Grocery stores throw out a lot of produce. Use that. Soups are good too. I know that's what is served at the charity kitchens. Drink more fluids, a lot of fluids, water and especially fruit juices."

Jon finishes up with a recommendation for an old and well proven medication, Bentil. It's an antispasmodic to calm the cramping.

I am stunned. What passed through me into Jon? How did we become one with the patient? I'm not the only one shocked.

* * *

"What did he do?" asked Kwang. He and Yoon were observing over a closed-circuit camera.

Dr. Yoon sat still as he processed what he'd seen. "When I was in school, I read of a man named Edgar Cayce. He was known as America's Mystic. He was able to do *readings* on people, medical readings. He had no medical training. Nobody understood how he did it, but he had a spectacular record of accuracy. Amazingly, he recognized the cause of the patient's problem and treated that rather than the symptom. His treatments were mostly holistic. Equally stunning was he did these *readings* remotely. People would write to him and set up a time and place where they would be. In his office, he would go into a trance and perform the *readings*."

Kwang stared at Yoon. "This guy was real?"

"He was, and it was proven, well documented." Yoon stares at Jon through the monitor window.

"I'm wondering if we have a new Edgar Cayce in Jon."

Chapter 36

I'm back in my realm. Instead of expanding outward, I'm in a cocoon blocking out everything. I have to think through what I've learned from Jon. And from Yoon and Kwang. I wasn't aware the Institute had a clinic. That the Institute is to be a medical facility to help all people is hard to fathom since I was sacrificed for the cause. The goal is glorious, but the means to get there is dark and dirty. I don't feel it was justified. The pain medication they are trying to synthesize will not be a processed and produced opiate and won't be subject to rigorous scrutiny like morphine. Endorphins are only a part of the body's pain-fighting. There is a whole spectrum of chemicals produced within the body, and as such there should be minimal side effects. The *high* drug users crave won't be there. But to torture me to death to get it?

I drift, letting this meander through my mind. Was I truly a convicted murderer? Was this an execution? How can I find out? If I were able to push Kwang or Yoon to look at the files…but I have had no success with that.

I pause. Does it really matter at this point? NO! I am what I am right now.

And then there's what happened with Jon. I learned something when that stream of energy flowed through me into him. We were linked at the time with something else. Perhaps he could have diagnosed the patient on his own, but I know I facilitated that *reading*. What a marvelous tool to see the energies and be inside of the patient–feel what they feel, sense what they sense. More than that, to become part of their body, seek out what it knows and does beyond the conscious mind. It was like an aerial view of a busy city with things moving everywhere and influencing everything else.

The complexity of this living thing was overpowering. Yet we were able to isolate parts and study them in detail, move along the paths of activity.

I know nothing about Edgar Cayce and have no way of researching him. Was he really a mystic? Yoon believes it. Is it possible he had someone like me or that stream of knowledge assisting him? I do like being able to help people. With my support, Jon can too.

Does anybody else in this realm of the afterlife do that? I break out of my cocoon and reach out with my mind. There are millions, no maybe billions of others. Chances are that other minds here can do that. Could connections exist in other areas beside medicine and health? Are some of the world's great engineers and inventers influenced by spirits?

A thought strikes me. Among these billions, I sense no young children. Where could they be? What happens to them that is different? Death is death. I have sensed the arrival of a new soul before. First there is nothing, then there is something, a new soul. But it is not a child's soul.

I've found adolescent souls, even pre-teen, but no young children's. Is there a cutoff? Why? Maybe it's not an age. Perhaps it is a state of mind, an awareness of the world. I do know that everyone here has some link to their previous life and the combination of all those billions of links forms another plane, or maybe dimension that exists with the world.

If someone isn't capable of or doesn't form that link, where do they go?

When I first arrived, I remember I had a choice to hold onto that connection or let it go. I kept it because that was a tie to the only world I knew—my only piece of familiarity. Where would I have gone if I had let it go?

Do I still have a choice? I begin to search for a soul who would let that link go. I want to find out what happens. I find one where the tie is weakening. What I sense is it fading out like a flashlight with dying batteries, growing dim. When the connection is gone, the spirit deflates like balloon with the air escaping. What is left is like ashes after a fire, then they blow away.

What happened? Where did the mind, the soul go? Is there no coming back from wherever it went. But then why would it want to? Little joy exists here, souls longing for what they cannot have. Maybe for eternity.

Is this truly a place where there is no time? Perhaps I will find the answer. I reach out with my mind seeking the destination of the soul that left here. There is something. It's like I'm window shopping, but the windows are frosted, not giving a clear view. I feel that on the other side of the glass is a dream, something spectacular, but I cannot go through to that other side.

My search for children continues, but proves fruitless. I discover something else instead. It is another soul–this one with a strong connection. It is firmly locked into the past life, reaching for it like a drowning man grasps at anything floating, but always out of reach–something it can never have. As I move into it, I feel the agony. This link is so strong, the desire so powerful, it will never be able to sever it.

The soul vanishes. I sense a flash of movement, but like a spark, it disappears. The link is like the trail of a bright shooting star that hangs in the sky before it fades. Where had this soul gone?

Apparently, this place is not a dead end.

Chapter 37

Kwang and Yoon are again watching Jon with another patient.

"Jon seems to be doing very well. Any word on his father?" asked Yoon.

"We lost track of him near Albuquerque. He discovered the tracker and the bug and put them on another vehicle. Our man checked on Leon when the tracker showed him in California. He wasn't there. We've started backtracking, trying to pick up a trail, but nothing so far."

"Do you think he's going to be a problem?"

Kwang shook his head. "More of an irritation at this point, but the risk could be high. He will try to contact Jon. We'll have to be vigilant."

Yoon nodded. "On a happier note, we're very close to synthesizing the compounds we need. I'm not sure we have to continue with the Extraction program.”

“That’s good news. I was never in favor of it, but we had no other way to get what we needed. Store the extractant and shut the program down.”

“We’ll keep looking for Leon though?”

Kwang nodded.

They turned to watch the session.

* * *

I’m in Jon

“What are you experiencing?” asked Jon of the patient.

“I have chest pains, shortness of breath and weakness in my left arm.”

Jon nods and approaches the table. She is pale and very overweight. Her legs are swollen.

The stream of knowledge passes through me into Jon. She becomes a system of energies. We enter the woman. The symptoms are as she described. We follow the circulatory system. The energy flow is slowed. The vessels have plaque restricting the flow of blood particularly in the heart. Jon studies the action of the valves.

He goes on to study the immune system. Her white blood cell count is a little low but not alarming. Her blood sugar is high. He looks at her liver. The energy seems adequate, but not fully healthy.

The energies of this woman are out of balance. The circulatory problems are like a traffic wreck slowing down activity in the city. The obesity is like overpopulation with everything crowded together creating pressure throughout. We pull out. He picks up his tablet and starts taking notes as he talks to her.

"You're a classic candidate for cardiac bypass surgery and valve replacement. Before we can do that, there are several things to do to ensure the surgery is a success. We will start you on a medication to reduce the plaque buildup. The condition you're in is due more to your lifestyle than genetics. This is your chance to change that."

"What do you mean?" she asks.

"To have a long-term benefit, you need to change your lifestyle, your habits and your diet. After the surgery, you will go to physical therapy every day to improve your circulation. You will be on a strict diet. You will start a gentle pool exercise program graduating from that to a more extensive program. You will get massages daily."

"I can't do that. I have things I have to do, kids and a business to run."

Jon shrugs "Then you will die."

Her mouth falls open.

"The decision is yours."

* * *

"We may need to work on Jon's bedside manner," said Yoon.

Chapter 38

I've left Leon alone for a while.

I do check on him occasionally. I'm with him now as he looks at the message he's encoded in an invoice. He'll send it via a remail drop center so it can't be traced back to him. If Jon is allowed to get the mail at the house, he'll get this. In code, the message says: *Mom is safe with your aunt, and I'm working.* He hopes they can be together again, but it won't happen for a while.

His short haul trucking job is working out fine, and he's found a small apartment. Since he left the Institute, he's had no nightmares. Barbara wants to join him at the end of the month. All of this is encoded in the invoice and service description of the company doing the invoicing, a real company in Salt Lake City. Until Jon is able to be alone to respond, the communications are one way.

I'm with Yoon and Kwang as they talk over what to do about Leon when they find him. The secret he holds is potentially too damaging to let him live. Unless he comes back to work for them.

"The boy is still going to the house?" asks Kwang

"Yes. He is accompanied. Jon picks up the mail, sorts it and pays bills. He is on the checking account. The utilities are on autopay, but there are a few bills that require him to write checks. Leon didn't want to give these companies access to his banking, so payments are the old-fashioned way."

"And we've examined the invoices and the payments?"

"Yes. One is a long-term care insurance policy and another is a real-estate company. Leon bought some vacant land in Utah. Both companies are legitimate.

"Leon did send two postcards to Jon. One was from Puerto Peñasco, Mexico. It's a small resort town on the Sea of Cortez. It was a brief message saying they were having a grand time on the beach. The other was from a resort near Tahoe, Nevada. It said much the same thing."

"Any way to see if they were really there?"

"We've checked it out. Inconclusive."

"It's been two weeks. We're going to have to do something."

Chapter 39

I'm reviewing the conversation Dr. Yoon had with Dr. Kwang about Edgar Cayce. "He had no medical training." Yet he was giving medical readings. How did he do that? How did he get that information? More importantly, how did he get that understanding?

I have no medical training, at least none I can remember. During my time with Jon while doing a reading, the connections with the patient passes through me. To see the patient as a balanced system of energies was fascinating, and did not start with Jon. I facilitated the connection, but I am not sure where it originated. I will have to investigate that extensively.

If it was a spirit that helped Cayce with the medical knowledge, where did that come from?

Was that spirit once a doctor? I go back to the soul that released the link to the past life and…left? disappeared? I need to find out.

I become conscious of my connection, something I haven't thought about for a while. I take it for granted and use it. I pause, unsure about reaching farther ahead. What's the downside? Will I be in a place less desirable than this one? I'm not sure that could be. Gradually, I let my attention to my connection fade and focus on what's ahead. I feel myself being drawn away as if I'm a piece of iron and a magnet is pulling me. My connection weakens and stretches like an elastic cord. The force pulling me grows stronger but I hold on to my link, not willing to finally give it up. I move through something, like a membrane and enter another realm.

Ahead of me is an immense mind. No! It is more like an endless ocean stretching out. I sense no end, no borders. It is a sea of knowledge, of understanding and…of love. If only I let go of my connection and then of myself, I will fall in and become a part of it. The desire to do that grows stronger, nearly impossible to ignore, yet I hold on. I reach out toward it. I am filled. It is an infinite library with all the answers to all the questions ever asked or ever will be asked. It is the understanding of everything. I am frozen in awe. My mind aches trying to understand everything.

The longing to stay with it is powerful, but slowly, I pull myself back, regretting doing so, wanting to join and be a part of it.

I now understand how I can help Jon. I need my connection with him.

Chapter 40

"Jon, have you heard from your father?" Dr. Yoon asks. They are preparing for another session in the clinic.

"I got a couple of postcards, but nothing else."

"Can you get in touch with him? We're getting a little concerned. He was supposed to be back last week."

"I tried to call, but his phone number is not working. I just thought he forgot to charge it. He does that sometimes. Should I be worried?"

"I don't think so. If you do hear from him, have him get in touch with us. We have an exciting new position for him." Yoon smiled.

"Let's proceed with the evaluation of the next patient."

I feel Jon's concern.

He isn't sure what to do. His father had made it clear the Institute might kill him and his mother to protect its secrets. Yet Dr. Yoon sounded like they wanted him back. He could encode a message in one of the checks he mailed out, but he hadn't received an invoice yet. Another payment wasn't due for a week. Caution, his father always said.

I also am torn as to what to do. I could do nothing and see how it plays out. I'll have to think on this a bit.

Jon and I will be diagnosing another patient in a few minutes. Yoon's questions about his father and mother bother him. He knows they are now together and doing okay. He doesn't know the location, but if he needs that information, he will be told. He doesn't know how sincere Dr. Yoon is about his father's return and another job for him.

The patient is a pregnant woman. The baby is not active and she is worried.

"How far along are you?" Jon asks.

"About seven and a half months."

"Have you been to another doctor?"

"No, but my mother is helping. She has experience with babies. She says everything is fine, but I'm not sure."

"Just relax and let me check."

I help Jon move into her.

As I am doing that, I reach back and create another connection to that sea of knowledge. A spirit flows through me and into Jon.

As Jon approaches the table, the woman becomes transparent layers of flowing energies. Jon can see everything. He studies the womb.

He speaks to the woman. "The baby has a nuchal." She stares at him, not understanding what that is. "The umbilical cord is wrapped around the baby's neck. This is not uncommon, but in this case, two wraps have occurred. This is restricting blood flow."

"How can that happen?" she asks.

"The baby moves around and in about thirty percent of births it occurs. Normally this isn't a concern if it is detected at birth, but in this case, the restricted blood flow can lead to problems with the baby. A cesarian section is justified, and since you're more than seven months along, we could do that soon. Is that what you want?"

"If it will save my baby, yes."

"I'll write this up and notify our operating room."

* * *

I am amazed at the diagnosis and Jon's knowledge, though I believe in great part, that comes from the connection I have with the spirit.

As Jon pulls out of the woman, the connection fades. Jon walks out of the examining room to find Yoon facing him.

"How did you find that without a scan?"

Jon shrugs. "I was able to see it."

"How?" asks Yoon again.

"When I approached the woman, her whole body appeared as if it was a scan. I could see everything about her. I could see circulation, skeleton, the nervous system, muscles, everything. I don't know why. It's what I saw. Actually, it was more what I felt."

Yoon looks puzzled. He recovers. "Elena will be doing the surgery. I'll be there, of course, but I want you in the OR too. If you sense anything we need to know, say something.”

“Sure. I’ll go get scrubbed.”

* * *

As soon as Jon left, Yoon was on the phone to Kwang. *I move into him.*

“Jon has done an amazing diagnosis on a woman needing surgery. He’s going to observe. Perhaps you should watch on the monitor.”

“When’s this going to take place?”

“They’re prepping her now.”

“It’s that serious?” asked Kwang.

“This is an opportunity for both Elena and Jon. The OR is vacant.”

I could feel Yoon’s excitement at this test of his two rising stars. He is a surgeon, and his presence is necessary under the operating permits for the clinic. And he wants to see them in action.

* * *

The woman is on the operating table. She has been given a spinal block rather than a general anesthetic. The robot surgeon is ready, and the site has been marked. Elena is watching a monitor, ready to stop the surgery or take over if she sees something incorrect. Jon stands beside the woman holding her hand, but he is looking at her abdomen.

I move into Jon and establish the connection.

Again, the woman is transparent. He watches the incision. In his vision, the instruments are not visible. The blood disappears as the suction tubes move it away.

The cut into the uterus begins and Jon says "Stop. The baby is directly under the cut." He reaches over and pushes the baby away. "Okay, resume."

The umbilical is double wrapped around the baby's neck. Carefully, Elena uncoils it and lifts the baby out. As soon as the cord is tied off, it is cut and the closing procedure starts. The robot does the suturing. Jon is amazed by the tiny stitches and the precision.

This is Jon's first operation. He feels satisfaction at the success and wonder at the procedure. I do too at the help I've supplied.

Yoon says nothing as he stands to the side observing. He thinks they must keep Jon at any cost.

Chapter 41

Leon looks at the payment statement and check he's received from Jon via the forwarding service. I can feel his relief at the message, It's straightforward on the surface. Jon's signature has a tiny ok like a curlicue. He'd sent a burner phone to Jackson, the guy he uses for yardwork, a long-time trusted employee, a week ago asking him to hold it for Jon. Leon's number was in the memory. The invoice number was the password. Now he needs to wait for Jon's call.

* * *

I'm with Jon.

He's at the house to get the mail. He's arranged for the yard guy to clean up. Alex is inside while Jon tells Jackson what's needed. As they walk out of sight of the front window, Jackson gives him the phone. With it in his pocket, Jon returns to the house.

"I need to stay here while this guy finishes."

Alex shrugs. "Doesn't matter to me. I go with you."

"You going in the bathroom with me?"

"Naw. You can handle that by yourself."

In the bathroom, Jon pulls out the phone and texts his dad. *Someone with me. Can't talk. U comg bk? Per K & Y you have new job here with the Institute. I'm doing med stuff. Really lv it. I try to get loose to talk when I can.*

He turns the phone off and hides it in the bathroom.

"Alex, we're going to be here a couple of hours. Let's go get some lunch."

Hamburger, fries and coke. He hasn't had that in a while. Alex has the same but the jumbo meal. As they finish up, Jon orders a meal for Jackson.

"Let's get back. I gotta pay some bills."

* * *

"Thanks," says Jackson. "I was getting hungry." Their eyes meet for a brief second.

Alex goes inside while Jon sits on the porch with Jackson as he eats.

Jon glances through the window at Alex watching a football game on TV. "Thanks for doing the work. Dad always thought you were good and fair." He points around to indicate possible mics picking up their conversation.

"Your dad always treats me well. Where are you staying?"

"I'm going to a boarding school not far from here. Dad set that up before they left."

Jackson glances at the window.

"The school takes student security seriously, so they have Alex come with me. Guess it's a legal thing." Jon stares at Jackson, his look saying that wasn't completely true.

"When are your mom and dad coming back?"

"I'm not sure. I know they needed a break, so this was good. I got a couple of postcards. They've been traveling. Don't know where they are now."

"Good thing you were able to take over the house care. The yard was a mess. If you need any handyman stuff, I could use the work."

"Thanks, I'll keep that in mind. I don't get here every day, so if you could stop by two to three times a week and water the plants, that would be good."

"Sure, no problem."

Jon rises. "I'll go write your check."

Inside, he sits at the kitchen table and fills out a check. He writes on a piece of note paper: *Thanks, see you in a few days to pay for watering,* and seals it in an envelope.

He watches Jackson leave after handing him the check. I feel his resentment at being watched all the time.

I also sense his worry about his parents' dilemma.

Chapter 42

I'm with Yoon and Kwang in the Kwang's office. I have to monitor these guys to see what they're going to do about Leon. As I become more familiar with them, getting into both of them as the same time is now easier.

"We've received no word from Jon's father?" asked Yoon.

Kwang shakes his head. "Neither has Jon, as far as we know. Our agent has not been able to locate them either. After Albuquerque, they dropped off the map."

Yoon pulls out a folder. "Our asset checked out the sites the postcards Jon received were sent from. He feels they were forwarded from a drop center. Leon wasn't there. If that's the case, it's looking like Leon won't be coming back. He may have suspected we considered his knowledge of our Extraction program dangerous to us."

"That may be especially true after we brought Jon in to live here at the Institute. I've been looking into Leon's history. He was in the army, stationed at Ft. Huachuca, Arizona in the intelligence section. Going back there would make sense. It's a place he knows."

Kwang nods. "I'll get word to the asset to go to Sierra Vista."

* * *

Eric Rumbel arrived in Sierra Vista midafternoon on Wednesday. It was a fair-sized town that grew up around Ft. Huachuca. After getting a room at the Southern Arizona Rancho - extended stay motel, he shopped the electronics stores. The base was an electronics support center for the army. The stores had stuff. His next task was to survey the electronic repair shops around town. Chances were that Leon would rely on his experience in intelligence section to get a job doing electronics repair.

At the seven shops listed for the town, he set up cameras linked to a monitor system in his room. He could watch all seven on a split screen. Once they were all working, he loaded a facial recognition program. By the time he had everything running, it was late. He went to bed. He'd check in the morning.

* * *

Three days passed, no hits. Leon wasn't working at those shops, if he was even here in this town. He'd leave the cameras while he figured where else seemed probable. He drove around on the weekend looking at neighborhoods. Kwang passed on the feeling that Leon would not be going back to the Institute, so probably he rented an apartment. As a military town, there were a lot of those.

Everyone had to buy groceries, so those were the next sites for cameras. If Leon's wife shopped, that would be a bust too. He didn't have a picture of her. Patience, he told himself. As long as Leon didn't suspect he was watched, he'd stay put.

Five days later, he got a hit. Leon had driven a box truck into one of the shops. The banner on the side of the truck was for a furniture shop. Eric retrieved his cameras and placed several outside of the store shown on the van's side. He waited.

Leon would show up in the morning and return in the afternoon. Some days, the truck would be unloaded at the store. Other days, it would be loaded in the morning and return a few hours later. He worked as a short-haul trucker, picking up furniture at the main warehouse in Tucson or delivering in Sierra Vista.

He had him.

* * *

I'm with Kwang and Yoon. "At least we know where Leon is," said Yoon. They were in Kwang's office. *I could feel their relief knowing Leon's location.*

"Is an *accident* in the future?" asked Kwang.

"I'd much rather have him back. Perhaps we should send him a message," said Yoon.

Kwang's hesitancy surprises me. "It would tip our hand and make other options harder."

"I do agree having him back would be the better option," pointed out Yoon.

I feel Yoon formulating a plan.

"Let's have the asset drop a note at his door. 'Leon, please come back to the Institute. Jon is doing well and we have another job for you here. Please contact us.' We'll let Eric decide what to do based on Leon's reaction."

"We will emphasize to Eric we prefer to have Leon back." Kwang smiled. "I like that. Unwritten, the note says 'We can find you.' And 'We have your son.' If he packs up to leave without calling, a car accident may be in order."

Chapter 43

Though I am able to enter Yoon and Kwang, I have not been able to influence them. Their conversation regarding Leon's future is troubling. I find this transformation from my overpowering desire for revenge interesting. I have changed. The link I have now is the desire to make things better.

I still don't understand what happens to the souls that depart from this existence, but I now believe this place is not permanent. Souls go elsewhere from here.

The dimension of Knowledge and Understanding is one destination. I'm not sure of the path to that, but I know it is an acknowledgement that self, ego, and the material life must be left behind. Only after one can accomplish that does the realm open. Why I am able to tap into it and transfer some of that knowledge I don't understand.

I suspect another path from here is when the soul is unable to progress. It enters another person, a baby, and lives another life. It's another chance to learn love, compassion and caring and shun the material attractions of the physical existence. It is what that past life is for. The temptations of greed, rank and status, possession of material things, hatred, jealousy, even the beauty of that world must be overcome. It is particularly difficult when I consider the genesis of human beings. All life on Earth is in competition for resources. How we overcome that seems impossible. It is in our genes.

If reincarnation is another path from this existence, it is a repeating one, and not really a departure, only the chance for one. The realm I am in is truly hell for most, as the things that dominated their past life do not exist here. My inability to remember anything of my past has eliminated those links.

* * *

Yoon is preparing Jon for another session. I am with them.

"Jon, I want you to diagnose a patient who is not physically present."

I feel Jon's confusion. "How can I do that?"

"The patient will be in the adjacent room. Imagine you are with him."

"I've never done anything like that." He pauses. "I'll try."

Yoon leads Jon into another examining room. "Lie on the table and just relax. The man is in the room next door."

I'm with Jon as he lies back.

Yoon uses a soothing voice to get Jon relaxed. Once he is calm, Yoon tells him to focus on the patient. *I push restful visions into his mind. Together we reach out. The image of the patient forms. We drift closer. Jon enters. I reach back to the dimension of knowledge and feel it flow through me into Jon.*

The man appears as layers if energies flowing around him. Jon is able to focus and separately view the circulatory system, the nervous system, the lymph system, the brain, the digestive system. He becomes the whole body with awareness of it in-depth.

Jon dictates the condition he has found. "The patient is suffering from liver disease. His lifestyle has damaged the organ. The damage is not fatal yet, but if the eating and drinking doesn't change, it will become so. He must avoid acetaminophen and Ibuprofen. Aspirin taken with food can be used for pain. Opioids if the pain becomes intense."

We withdraw. Yoon is standing beside the examining table. "That was wonderful, Jon. Do you think the distance from the patient is a factor?"

"There was no distance involved. With your description of the location, I found the patient. Once I connected, I was able to enter."

"Jon, many years ago a man named Edgar Cayce was able to give medical readings. What you are doing seems quite similar. I would suggest you look into him. The information is available in our database. I'll forward the links."

This will be my opportunity to learn more about this man. I withdraw from Jon. Back in the realm of souls, I reach out again for the center of knowledge. It is closed to me.

Chapter 44

Leon's hand is shaking so badly he can't read the note. *I feel his terror and anger.* The note was taped to his door. The first time he read it, his heart seemed to stop. The second time, he couldn't believe it, the third time, he rushed to the door to see if anyone were there. The ·fourth time, he resigned himself to returning to the Institute. The threat was in the note.

He reaches for his phone and steadies his voice. "Dr. Yoon, this is Leon Prosky. I want to let you know I will be returning next week. My vacation got extended, but I am coming back."

"Thank you, Leon. We look forward to having you back at work. I'm happy to say Jon is excelling, and we are very happy to have him here. We'll meet on Monday. Drive safely."

Leon tells his wife the news. He holds out the note. She gasps as she reads it. The knowledge they know where he is, the veiled threat they have Jon.

Next, he calls the furniture company to say he has a family emergency and he must resign. He calls the apartment manager and explains he will be leaving before the end of the week.

Barbara looks at him as he's finishing the calls. "Do you think they really want you back?"

"It doesn't matter. We have to go. If they were going to kill us, it would make more sense to do it here rather than close to the Institute. They have Jon." Leon texts Jon they would be coming back over the weekend.

* * *

Eric Rumbel watched Leon and his wife prepare to move. They didn't have much to pack, and were ready to leave by the end of the day. He had placed a tracker on the car and a bug inside. They had discovered the others previously, and may find these and remove them. He would be following them. Any sign they were trying to make a break, and he would act.

* * *

Kwang taps on his desk. "You believe Leon is coming back?"

Yoon nods. "We hold the cards. He'll be here. The question is in what capacity. We've shut down the Extraction Program."

"Let's continue with his medical training. It will be a good test of our training program. Leon is not the ideal student for a medical career. If he can learn enough to make him a med tech or aide, it would be good."

"Yes," said Yoon. "He has electronics aptitude. Perhaps we could use him in maintenance and repair of our robots while he's training."

Kwang nods. "How's Jon doing?"

"Yesterday I tried him at remote reading. He passed with flying colors. Jon will be a tremendous asset to the clinic."

"What's remote reading?"

Yoon smiled. "Jon was able to diagnose a patient without being physically in the room with him."

Kwang's expression showed his surprise. "And he's accurate?"

Yoon nodded.

"How do you see us using him?"

"Here at the clinic, he can diagnose many patients in a short period of time. He can also diagnose patients who make a remote appointment. We can then offer treatment at the clinic. Between Jon's abilities and our own automated systems, we can treat many patients every day."

"Where are we on the new pain medication?"

"We have synthesized the first batch and will test it this week. Chemically, it is indistinguishable from the natural extractions. The process is not cheap, but we will automate it within the next two months."

"How are our other students doing?"

"Elena has become extremely deft in automated surgery. She would be an exceptional surgeon at even the best hospitals. We are rotating students from the university medical school. They will renew our contract and have already asked about expanding past the four students we take at a time."

"We must not over extend," commented Kwang. "As long as we remain a small operation, the large facilities don't see us as competition and regulatory agencies are satisfied. The last thing we need is governmental *help*."

"That brings up another point," said Yoon. "Our patients will talk. Eventually the media will get wind of us. We need to be ready to handle that unwanted attention."

"We could require non-disclosure agreements before we treat."

Yoon shook his head. "That's only a temporary stop. The agreements will attract attention by themselves."

"What's your solution?"

"I don't know. We'll have to think on this."

Chapter 45

I'm with Jon as he reads the files Yoon forwarded to him about Edgar Cayce. What a fascinating man he was. Without any medical training, he accurately diagnosed maladies in hundreds of patients. His treatments were holistic and dealt with the causes, not the symptoms. The patient would set the time and place. Cayce would go into a trance and make the reading.

Some of his theories seem pretty wild, like an advanced civilization in Atlantis and the five different races. When asked how he was able to make these readings, his answer was like a blinding light to me. He said a spirit entered him during his trance and made the readings.

Was this what I was doing with Jon? It would seem so. It wasn't unique. I also believe more contacts between the place I am in now and the world of my past life exist. Is it possible spirits help in other areas like science and engineering? Are other geniuses influenced? What is exceptional with me is I'm not in the torment most of the other souls here are trapped in. Why?

With no memory of my past, the only tie I had was to my torturer and my killer. That link has expanded to others, but also the drive for revenge against Jon and Leon has faded. I am not in strife. Others must exist in this realm also.

The other interesting thing I've encountered is religious souls. The souls are individual, but, like iron particles attracted to a magnet, they seem to group. I don't believe they connect with each other.

Instead of links to past lives holding them back, they are blocked by false ideals. It is ironic that the carrot used to bring them into the folds of the religion is the thing keeping them from attaining Heaven or Paradise.

Is that dimension of knowledge, understanding and love I encounter Heaven or Paradise? I feel it is. One only enters when all ego from the past life is left behind. It is the raw soul that becomes a part of it. In doing so, there is no individual any more. I have not given up my sense of self, and thus could not join, but I am allowed to tap into it. Why?

It is not the description used to attract followers. Seeking that goal of Heaven or Paradise only prevents them from achieving it.

Chapter 46

I decide to try to get more information from the center of knowledge. The connection seems to be one-way, and not necessarily initiated by me. I can act as a transport of information from it into Jon. In the past when I tried to enter to get more information, I was blocked.

I'm not sure what this means.

When I make contact, that dimension seems like a single entity. That word isn't right, but I can think of no other. When one is in the ocean, it seems to be a single thing, yet it is made up of individual molecules of water. It flows around you, pushes you, surrounds you. But it is not a single thing. There are currents separate from others but influencing the whole. When I reach out to this entity, a current from it flows through me into Jon. The information goes to Jon, not to me, but since I am in Jon, I see what he sees.

To make the connection, I feel as if I'm going through a portal. The ocean of this next realm is on one side, and mine is on the other. It's much the same with the life I came from. On one side is the physical world. On the other is where I am. I can return to the physical only through a connection with a mind. I have no real presence and must experience it through the senses of people. The transition from that physical world to here is one-way. Unless souls return into other physical bodies. Reincarnation?

Do they carry memories with them?

I do think the soul is the record of life, maybe the record of multiple lives. But that record is not in the conscious mind of the individual. Can it be tapped into? Some claim so. I don't know. I do think the soul influences the subconscious.

Access to my past records is blocked by my ego. If I release that sense of myself, perhaps my soul will be open to me, but who would I be?

I have sensed the links from the souls here extending back into the physical world. Most of those links are tying memories of the physical life to the soul. Without the ability or desire to release that connection, souls are trapped because they try to live in the physical, which does not exist here.

The portal from the physical to this existence is death. I am an exception. Probably not the only one.

Is the same true of the transition from here to the next realm?

I expand my sense of mind outward seeking that ocean. Something is here, but it is like air in the physical world—unseen, yet felt only when there is movement. If the existence in my realm is a dimension separate from the physical world, is this next realm another dimension? Are there multiple layers, each an expansion, one encompassing another? Does this next realm influence the one I am in? Does it decide when a soul must return from here to the physical?

Based on my experience with this next realm, I think only a pure soul is allowed to merge. It must be free of the ego of the last life. It cannot merge and remain an individual.

This realm I am in is not the hell of eternal fire described by the religions. The torment is being adrift in a place with no anchor. It is the last chance to go forward or, for those hopelessly tied to the material world, go back.

Chapter 47

Jon reads the text from his father. At first, he feels joy at his parents' return. Doubt at the sincerity of Dr. Yoon's and Dr. Kwang's offer of a new job and a place at the Institute creeps in. He realizes the decision by his father to return has to do in part with him being here.

I have sympathy for Jon's dilemma. He has found a place, something he truly enjoys doing to replace the feelings of inadequacy he had in the past. He is useful and helping people. The aims to lower medical costs and cover more people are heroic. The Extraction Program was not.

I am with him as he's doing another remote reading this morning. He has learned to rapidly enter into a trance-like state. He lies back, letting his mind drift. With a push from me, he focuses on the patient. I open the connection to the realm of knowledge.

I am like a pipeline only transferring the flow. What I am aware of is like a reflection bouncing back from Jon as I join with him. Without me, I'm not sure he could achieve the level of focus needed. He does seem to be learning. Possibly, he may not need me in the future, but that time is not now.

Jon finishes his diagnosis and withdraws. Yoon stands beside the examining table. "The diagnosis was good. Are you doing well?"

"Yes," says Jon.

"We have another patient."

"I need a break, something to drink and a bathroom."

"Sure, Jon. It's nearly lunchtime. Go on down to the cafeteria. We'll start up when you're done eating."

* * *

The table Jon and Elena sit at is not near the others.

"How are you doing, Jon? You seem tired."

Jon looks at his plate, moving the food around without eating. "I got a text. My parents are coming back."

"You don't seem very happy at the news."

I feel his discomfort. He can't say anything negative about the Institute.

"I'm just tired." His smile is weak. He changes the subject. "How are you doing?"

Elena's smile is bright. "The surgery has been busy. The AI is good, the mechs are learning. I'm observing mostly, but concerned what would happen if there's a breakdown. They are machines. Before I could intervene, a serious mistake could be made."

"Has a breakdown happened?"

"Not in a long time. The mechanical surgery equipment does a continuous self-diagnosis."

"What would happen if a human surgeon made a mistake?"

Elena stares at him for a moment. "The mistake would be corrected as best it could and then everything covered up." She shrugs. "That part of the medical profession hasn't changed. It certainly will with robotic surgeries."

"Have my diagnoses helped?"

"They've been right on. How do you do that?"

"I'm not sure how to explain. It's like I can get inside a patient." Elena's expression shows she doesn't understand. "When I'm with them, they're not flesh and bone. They are flowing energies of different systems." He pauses, seeing Elena's confusion.

"For example, I can select the circulatory system and it opens before me. Anything wrong changes color and I can look closer. I can switch to the digestive tract and the same thing happens."

"Wow!" Elena stares at him. "I've never heard of anything like that."

"Lately, I have been able to do the readings remotely, without being with the patient. Many times, when I sense imbalances, I can recommend holistic changes, like diet."

"What's your procedure when you do these readings?"

"I go into a restful trance, and I'm directed to the patient."

"Directed?"

"I don't' know how else to put it. I've been reading about another guy who did stuff like this back in the nineteen-thirties up until the nineteen-fifties. His name was Edgar Cayce. It's a pretty fascinating story. I'll send you the files."

Elena smiles. "I'm not sure when I'll be able to read them, but please do." She rises and picks up her tray. "I have another surgery in a few minutes. Can we talk more later?"

Jon nods. He eats a few bites, picks up his tray and leaves it at the bussing station.

Chapter 48

Leon knew he had a tail, probably the guy who left the note in Sierra Vista. During a quick stop in Albuquerque, he had managed to lose him long enough to drop off his wife. She could stay with her sister again. Until he was sure things at home were okay, he wouldn't have to worry about her. She could join him later.

Pulling into his driveway, he noticed the house looked pretty good. Jackson had kept it up. The first thing he did was to search out the cameras and bugs. He left them in place, used a frequency finder to tap into the signals. The bugs would now work for him also. He could block or alter the signals if he wanted to. A central control location was needed. He disabled one of the Institute's cameras by pulling a wire loose.

He called the Institute. "Dr. Yoon, I'll be in Monday."

"Great to hear, Leon. We look forward to having you back."

"Could I pick up Jon? I'd like to have dinner with him."

"Sure. He'll be finished with his sessions about five."

* * *

Leon had checked for cameras in his garage, but hadn't found any. It was one place without CCTV, but probably had microphones. He emptied a large cabinet and installed the control panel for his monitoring equipment in the back. He could tap into any of the Institute cameras in his house to see what they were recording. He made loop tapes from each room that could substitute for the real view. He set up his own alarm system to alert him if anybody entered. Placing a panel in front of his equipment, a false front of shelves, his system would be hidden. By the time he finished, it was time to pick up Jon.

* * *

For an awkward moment they faced each other before Leon gave Jon a hug.

Hey, Dad, it's good to see you."

"Good to be back. Let's go get some pizza."

In the car, Leon pointed up, circled his finger and then pointed to his ear to signal they were being monitored. "I understand you're doing well. Tell me about your sessions."

"I'm not sure what happened, but now I'm able to get into a patient and diagnose their problems."

"How does that work?"

"When I focus on the subject, I see all the systems of the body. I can separate them into the different ones and then combine them."

Leon gave his son a puzzled look.

"Let's say you have a pain in your arm. I can look at the bones to see if there's a fracture, the muscles to see if there's a tear, or the nerves to see the source of the pain."

"You can do all that? How?"

"Something inside me changes, gives me a new vision. It's not one of the usual senses, like touch, smell, sight or the others, yet at times it seems to be all of them combined and more."

"You can do that just by being with the patient?"

"I don't have to be with them anymore. I can project myself to wherever they are."

"No wonder they like you so much." Leon turned into the parking lot of a small strip center and found a spot near the restaurant. "We're here. I'm really hungry."

"I haven't had pizza in a while. The food at the Institute is good, but I miss the junk food."

The restaurant was geared for kids and a wall of noise hit them as they entered.

"You sure you want to go here?" asked Jon.

"No bugs work in here," said Leon.

Leon led Jon to a table near a large family. "What do you not want on your pizza?"

Jon laughed. "Anchovies."

"Okay, I'll get a deluxe." He rose. "Drink?"

"Cola."

In the line for the order counter, Leon watched the people around Jon. It was mostly the kids at the next table. He surveyed the room. One man sat at a table by himself. He was stocky, with closely cropped hair. He looked away as Leon gazed at him.

Leon filled two glasses with their drinks and returned to the table. He placed their order number card in the holder. "Should be here in a few minutes."

"Dad, are you being paranoid?"

"It's only paranoia if it's not true. I'm not ready to throw all my trust behind these guys again."

"Uh, okay. Where's Mom?"

Leon placed his hand in front of his face as if scratching his nose. "She's with her sister. If everything's kosher, she'll come back in a few weeks. If Yoon asks on Monday, I'll know they're watching. I'll tell him she stayed in Sierra Vista for a while."

Jon regarded him for a second. Their pizza arrived.

Chapter 49

I'm with Jon as he's in a trance in his observation room. He is diagnosing a pregnant mother about to give birth in another room. He senses her through the connection I hold with the realm of knowledge. I now think of it as a spirit that travels through the connection I open. His vision reveals the baby will not survive the birthing. Its malformed-lungs will not be able to sustain it. The condition would require a lung transplant. Not possible here. Contractions begin.

I watch through Jon. I also sense another soul. This one has none of the characteristics of those in my realm, but they are tied to their past lives. This one is like a freshly erased chalkboard awaiting the opportunity to enter the baby. As the baby emerges, it is a stillbirth. I am fascinated as I sense the soul hovering. It draws away. Part of me follows. It moves to another birth, another baby. With the first breath, the soul enters. I sense all of this in a place with no dimensions, no time.

One of my questions is answered. But where did the soul come from? Is it from that realm I am in but returning to the physical world because it was unable to move on? Is it a new soul with no past? If so how did that happen? I feel this other dimension oversees the place where I am AND the physical world. Are there more worlds?

Does this next dimension manipulate the physical world? The answer is in that body of knowledge. Once I join with it, there are no questions, only answers. I had assumed it was a one-way trip. There would be no me anymore. It is what all the souls in my realm strive for. Why do I hesitate?

What if that dimension manipulates the perception of the physical world?

What if the physical world is only perception?

Jon pulls me back from this line of thought. The stillbirth disturbs him. He has changed from the mopey teen with little regard for life other than his own to someone with empathy. He rises from the examining table and paces the room. Yoon enters.

"Jon, we cannot save everyone."

I slip into Yoon's mind. He is genuinely concerned for Jon, who represents a leap for medical care at the Institute's clinic.

"Dr. Yoon, I'd like to have lunch with my dad. Is that possible?"

An image of Leon forms in Yoon's mind. Keeping Jon's loyalty to the Institute depends on Leon. Yoon considers the father a risk, a loose end but perhaps a necessary one. "Sure. He's attending instructions on robot maintenance. I'll get a message to him to meet you in the cafeteria."

Jon wants to meet where it's possible for them to talk, but an objection wouldn't be good. "Thanks."

There is a dark side to Yoon's thoughts about Leon. I feel he is looking for an opportunity to get rid of him as long as it won't cause a problem with Jon.

* * *

I am with Jon as sits at a table. Elena walks up and asks if she can join him. Despite his annoyance at not being alone with his dad, he says yes.

Elena puts her hand on Jon's arm. "I understand the delivery didn't go well."

Jon frowns and stares at the table. "The baby was never viable. Its lungs were massively deformed. If I had been able to give a reading early in the pregnancy, I would have recommended an abortion."

"It happens, Jon. The first patient I lost was hard on me."

Leon walks up. Jon stands. "Hey, Dad, I'd like you to meet Elena. She's doing medical training here with me. This is my dad, Leon. Elena is a surgeon."

She laughed. "Well, not yet, but I'm working on it."

Leon holds out his hand. "Pleased to meet you. I don't get a lot of time to eat, so I should probably get my lunch." He walks to the food line.

Jon rises. "We should probably eat too."

When they were seated again, Elena asks, "Leon, how long have you been here at the Institute?"

"Several years, but I worked in another area. They recently moved me to robot and machine maintenance. I'm in training now."

"Glad to hear that," says Elena. "We depend on the machines so much. If something goes wrong, people might die."

"Do you live here at the Institute?"

"I do. What about you?"

"I'm living in our house." He glances at Jon. "It's not far." As Leon begins to eat, the conversation dies.

Jon wonders about his mother's visit with his aunt. He was unaware they had communicated. His mom never spoke of her sister, Ginger. He can't remember much about her, though he did meet her as a child.

His mom's stay with her is his dad being cautious.

Chapter 50

In his garage, Leon opened the panel in his cabinet to reveal his home monitor system. He checked the alarms. This morning while Leon was at work, someone rang the doorbell, then knocked when there was no answer. He picked the lock on the front door, entered the house and shut off the alarm. *How did he know the code?*

Leon scrolled through the video. It was the same man who had been at the pizza place when he and Jon had dinner.

He reviewed the recordings as the intruder checked the house room by room looking at the cameras he had planted. The disabled one was replaced. It's what drew the man inside where Leon could see him.

Was he looking for signs of Leon's wife also? That issue had not come up during the interview after his return. They were watching him.

* * *

"Your dad seems nice," said Elena. "But he's pretty quiet."

"We didn't talk much at home."

"What did he do before he started the maintenance training?"

Jon stared at her a second before looking down at his tray. *I can't say anything about the basement even if she's here at the Institute also.* "He was in an area developing new products. I don't know exactly. He couldn't talk about it."

He smiled at her. "I've got to get back soon—more readings to do. You have any other surgeries today?"

"I'm on call. Can I watch you do a reading?"

"It's okay with me, but we should check with Dr. Yoon."

* * *

Elena looked around the bare room. There was a chair, an examining table, and not much else. A video camera was mounted in one corner near the ceiling. They were in Jon's observation room.

"Elena, mute your pager. If you get an alert, try to leave without making a disturbance," said Dr. Yoon. "I'll be in the next room. Signal me if you need anything." He closed the door as he left.

I'm with Jon for the reading. "This is the first time I've done a reading with anyone other than Dr. Yoon present," said Jon.

A monitor of the adjacent room shows a middle-aged man as he comes in and stretches out on the examining table. He is slightly overweight with thinning hair. Jon lies down and closes his eyes. Elena watches as his breathing slows.

I try to enter Elena and find it very easy. She is open and trusting. Her mind is fresh as she seeks to understand what Jon is doing. The balance between being a conduit for the spirit into Jon and being in Elena is delicate but gets easier as the reading progresses.

The body of the man on the table becomes layers of energies to Jon as he begins to read it. One area glows red–gallbladder. It is hotter than the tissues around it. The nerves are transmitting pain. That is probably the main cause of the man's distress, but Jon continues to read him. A duct from the liver is restricted.

Elena is fascinated by the inert figure in adjacent room. She sees nothing happening until Jon's eyes open.

He looks over at her. "You need to prep. He needs surgery." He relates the results of his reading to her.

I withdraw from Jon and stay with Elena. I haven't been through a surgery before.

* * *

With the patient prepped and in the OR, Elena reviews the surgery in her head. She will be overseeing the robot operations to catch any problems, but these are fairly straightforward.

Upon entering, she inspects the anesthesiologist robot. Displayed on a monitor is the patient's weight and body mass, the anesthesia to be used and the dosage. Other medications he had taken were also displayed along with alerts.

Another monitor shows respiration, blood pressure, and pulse rate.

At the operating table, Elena inspects the patient. She speaks some reassuring words to him then tells him, "Count backward from one-hundred." With a touch on a panel, the patient's eyes close by the time he reaches ninety-three. She looks at the monitors until she's satisfied he is under.

With another touch, scalpels on robot arms descend and make tiny incisions. Small probes enter the cuts. One is a camera feeding images directly to the surgical probe. Another expands the abdomen with gas to make it easier for the surgical probe to work. Elena thinks this is a typical laparoscopic cholecystectomy to remove the gallbladder, except it is being performed by machines.

With that complete, the probe moves on to the blocked duct. A stint is fed in and the blockage bypassed. The robot surgeon beeps, a signal it is finished and ready to close. Elena approves.

Through her eyes, I watch the patient moved to recovery. The surgery was fast and efficient. After cleaning up, she goes to her apartment. I can feel her exhaustion. Though she oversaw the operation, the stress factor of intense observation and being ready to take over in an instant has tired her. She wants a short nap before joining Jon for dinner.

Chapter 51

As Elena dozes, I wander through her memories. Mostly they are of her time here at the Institute. Her medical lessons were like those Jon had, but the technology is better now. Still, she has the talent and drive to be a doctor. She truly enjoys what she is doing, helping people. Her memories of the Institute, and her life here are wonderful, but her earlier life is locked behind a very solid door. I sense whatever is behind that door is pain.

I watch as the door in her memory seems to bulge inward under forces trying to get out. A crack develops and a black tendril worms through. She moans and slams the portal shut. There be monsters there. I withdraw back to my realm.

Elena suffers from PTSD. As long as she is able to keep the doorway sealed, she is fine. Eventually, parts will sneak through. I don't know if I can help her, but I am determined to try. I reach out to the next realm.

Traumatic events cause emotional distress. I know that first hand. What helped me is the realization that those events cannot harm me here. I no longer am a part of the physical world…unless I choose to visit it through another person. First, I will have to find out what is within the chamber she seals off.

I rejoin her. She is in the cafeteria having dinner with Jon.

"Jon, your diagnosis was exactly correct. Explain again how you did that?"

"When I go into the trance, I visit the body, but not in the usual sense. Instead of a lump of flesh and bundles of bones, I see energies, sensations, nerves, all the parts. I sense what makes up the body. There is a balance to it. When a part is not in balance, I am able to see that."

"You saw the gallbladder?"

"What I saw was an imbalance that was causing an intense glow. Where a normal body would be like a concert with everything in harmony, there was a disturbance. It's like a smooth flowing stream with something causing ripples. That's the only way I can describe it. I follow that until I can understand what's causing it."

"You also saw the blockage in the duct."

"It was like another rock in the stream, another wrong note in the concert."

"Can you take these readings on anybody?"

"I'm not sure. I think so."

Elena gazes at Jon for a few seconds. "Could you do one on me?"

Jon studies her. "Is something wrong with you?"

"Physically, I'm fine."

"And?"

"Sometimes I have dark thoughts, terrifying thoughts." She looks down at her tray. "They wake me up at night. My heart is racing, screams want to come out, but I clamp my hand over my mouth to keep them in."

"I've never tried to do anything other than physical readings." His mind whirls at the concept of someone else having horrible dreams. "I've had nightmares sometimes too."

The image of me on the shock table jumps up.

"What are the dreams of?" Jon asks.

"I don't know. My emotions rise up and overpower my vision like a tsunami. I don't see what is flooded, only the wave covering everything."

"We can try it."

* * *

This will be interesting. Jon doesn't enter the mind of his subject. But I do.

In Jon's room, Elena gets on the bed, Jon lies on the floor. He closes his eyes and reaches out to her. I open the conduit. The spirit reaches out to her. Her body is the concert of biological operations, but the spirit only sees her body. It doesn't enter her mind.

I do.

The doorway is before me, pulsing from the thing inside trying to force its way out. A crack forms. I dart inside.

Horrible images of men executing her parents as they kneel. The explosive roar of the guns echos around the room. There is little blood, as the head shots kill them before they fall to the floor. The men are faceless looming black shadows. She ducks under one as it reaches for her and runs outside. More black demons are murdering her whole village—men, women, children all kneeling in the plaza. The air is filled with their screams and crying, silenced by the reports from the guns. She runs in a panic, her only destination is to be away from it all.

Later, she knows not how long, she feels a man reach down to her body curled on the ground among the stalks of maize. She squeezes her eyes tightly shut.

It is no wonder she cannot see this memory. This didn't happen to me but if I had a stomach, I would be vomiting everything I'd eaten for the last week onto the ground. How can I help her? I flee from this place.

An idea forms. I replay the scene, but I turn the characters into animated cartoon figures. There is no blood. Clowns are using squirt guns. Townspeople with water pistols are running and laughing. The buildings are made of cake. Mounds of ice cream are heaped to one side. Candy canes line the street. It's a Candyland scene. Will Elena ever be able to view this event?

I begin to play it like a cartoon with cartoon music in her head. I feel her tense, but she pushes the emotion down. She watches.

Chapter 52

I am back in my realm. Is it possible I am able to help people suffering from PTSD? I was able to move into Elena without difficulty. Perhaps it is getting easier for me to enter others. I try Yoon again. Entering him has become less difficult. He is in a meeting with Kwang. I am now able to enter Kwang at the same time. They are in a discussion about Leon.

"Leon is struggling in the equipment maintenance department," says Yoon. "Much has changed since he was in the Army. If he were a new recruit, we would not keep him on."

Kwang sighs. "But we want to keep Jon, so we need to have Leon here. Has Jon's mother returned?"

"Our surveillance cameras have not picked her up. She is elsewhere."

"Where?" asked Kwang.

"On the drive back, Leon made a stop at a restaurant in Albuquerque. His wife did not return to the car when he left. If she is there, we have no information about any relatives or friends."

"Our asset had to stay with Leon. Send someone and start a search for her. As a loose end, we need to know where she is."

"Yes, sir."

Unsaid but in both of their minds was the idea they would have to get rid of Leon and his wife.

"We need to restart the Extraction program," says Yoon. "Our efforts to synthesize the material from the subjects worked, but it is not as effective as it should be. There are other factors involved. Whether it is other chemicals or not, we need to find out."

"We have Leon. and he was very good at extractions," said Kwang.

"I'll let him know he's going back to his old job."

* * *

Jon and Elena sit at a table in the cafeteria having lunch. A nearby table has four med students from the university. They are excited by the Virtual Reality lessons.

"I can't believe how realistic it is," gushed one girl. "It's like being inside of the body."

"It's better than dissection in the anatomy classes. Everything is labeled," said another. "The complexity of the body is in separate lessons making it much easier to comprehend."

"I've heard they will add the lessons together in layers," said another.

* * *

Jon looked at Elena. "I probably didn't help you at all."

She smiled. "It did something. In the last couple of days, the dreams aren't scary."

"When I did your reading, everything seemed to be all right. Nothing was abnormal. But then, I only sense the body, not the mind."

"I now realize what I was suppressing was the memory of my parents' deaths. It remains traumatic, but now I can at least think about them without being buried under emotion. It's getting better."

Maybe I can help? It seems so, at least in Elena's case. I would have to enter the subject. That may not always be possible and takes time.

Chapter 53

After listening to Jon and Elena, I need to become more familiar with Yoon and Kwang. Their apparent altruistic motives seem a little too good to be true. I haven't been able to project into either of them, but having spent more time in Yoon, I feel as if I'm closer.

Yoon is in his office with Leon.

"Leon, we need to restart the Extraction program."

I feel Leon's discomfort at the idea. In the time since he left, he has allowed more empathy into his mind. "I can do it, sir, although I would prefer to stay with the maintenance program."

"We have no one else trained."

"When do you need to restart the program?"

"Next week."

"Can you train somebody else?"

"Leon, you were very good. We cannot have anyone else ready in that short time."

I feel Yoon's concern at Leon's hesitation.

"I'll do it, sir, though I hope it's not permanent."

"Thank you, Leon." Yoon rises to signal the meeting is over.

I stay with Yoon. His mental control is like an iron fist. Though I have not been able to project into him, I keep prying. I attempt to explore his memory. A series of images appear like flipping through a photo album with flashes of events from the past. They seem to be in a chronological order as the figures age. An image of a woman talking to him appears. She is Asian and speaks a language I cannot understand. I press forward and the images scroll by as he grows older. I stop at one where he is receiving a certificate. The writing is nothing I can read. I continue to scroll as Yoon appears in a laboratory in a white coat. He is opening a package with English writing on it. The label on the vial reads **varicella-zoster virus**. I don't know what that is.

In a later image, he is looking at a monitor with a picture of a lumpy ball with hair-like spikes coming out of it. The virus from the package, I think. In another mage he is using a tool with beams of light to make changes to the ball. I suspect he has modified the virus.

I do not know where he was or when these memories were formed. I continue to scan. He is receiving an award in another ceremony. In a different scene, a man in military uniform is talking to him, in a small office. They are alone, but I cannot understand what they are saying. They shake hands.

Two uniformed soldiers and the man who was talking to him are in a vehicle driving through a forest. Another scene: He is on a trail moving through the trees. He approaches a fence. The next image shows the fence behind him as he moves away. He has crossed a border of some sort. I scan quickly ahead until an image of Kwang appears.

So much of this I do not understand—the language, the laboratory, the writing. I have no resources to help unless…the body of knowledge. Would it be possible for me to make contact with it as more than a conduit of information to Jon?

As when I'm establishing the conduit to Jon, I reach out into another dimension and reach for the effervescent cloud. I touch it. I had been blocked before, but not this time.

I am swept away as an endlessness of knowledge opens up before me. Part of it is a physical universe, the one I was in, I think. But instead of vast emptiness with the lights of galaxies, it is a sea filled with other energy and matter.

Lines of force flow. What I had viewed as galaxies before are more than concentrations of brilliant lights. Lines of force, gravity, are also concentrated within them. At the center the lines form a tube going somewhere else. It's not really a tube because there are more dimensions to it than the three I knew. Around it, I see different levels with transitions between them.

Another layer, not the physical realm but mental trails of thought, layers upon layers. It is a tapestry of infinite threads woven together and interacting—moving and shifting. The tapestry is expanding. Threads that extend outward are weaving themselves together. I understand the growth outward is the move through time. The future relies on the past and is created by the probabilities of the threads coming together.

There is no random. When the base is infinite, all possibilities are included. What humans see as chance is the inability to see everything. I feel as if my mind is exploding. Colors I've never known surround me. It is overwhelming.

I pull back and focus on the images of Yoon's memory.

A plot, a single thread, plays out. I follow it.

Yoon is Korean—born and educated in North Korea. He received degrees in medicine and virology research. The **varicella-zoster virus** is his specialty. He has modified this Shingles virus to make the nerve inflammation much more intense.

I cannot remember anything of the physical world, yet his flight from North Korea seems to be part of a bio-weapon program under the North Korean regime. The virus was modified to become more contagious and attack the nerves as Shingles does. Its surface characteristics were not the same. Shingles vaccines like Shingrix wouldn't activate the body's immune system to fight it.

I am stunned. Western medicine would not be able to fight this, to contain an outbreak. I continue following the thread.

This particular strain developed by Yoon remains inert in the body, undetectable and doing nothing, much like Shingles. People become infected and pass it on without anyone knowing. Why? What is the purpose? I continue to follow. There's more information. In the presence of another chemical, it becomes active.

In the years since Yoon left North Korea, he and other agents introduced this virus into countless people. It has now spread through much of the world. Remaining inactive. Nobody knows. Yoon is proud of what they have accomplished.

Research and development continued at the North Korean laboratory. A vaccine has been created. Of what use is a vaccine against a virus that is inactive? The plan is nefarious and ingenious. The activating chemical will be added to a common fertilizer used globally. It will enter the food chain.

The economic disaster created by COVID was a lesson, a roadmap to destroy the economies of nations. And a plot to raise North Korea to a global power. The Shingles X disease does not kill, but it disables. The medical profession will be overwhelmed worldwide by people suffering from this.

As the sole supplier, North Korea will sell the vaccine globally. As economies are collapsing, theirs will soar. It is a path to becoming a superpower. Not a shot will be fired, not a soldier will be killed.

I try to follow Yoon's thread outward beyond the weaving. Other threads are moving toward it. The plan grows, but another thread appears. It is different, like a fiberoptic thread, transparent, not as solid as the others. It weaves itself into the plan and scatters the weaving.

I try to follow that thread back to see its past, but unlike others emerging from the past of the tapestry, the thread starts recently and is short.

Despite a powerful urge to release from myself and stay within this realm and become a part of it, I withdraw. I am stunned by the immensity of Yoon's plan. But the strange thread changed it. I am exhausted by my exploration.

But why is Yoon so interested in Jon?

As a scientist, he is driven to understand. I also suspect it is not only because Jon is able to read patients but might detect the virus and become a threat to the master plan. If his readings detect the virus, it would offer time for a western development of a vaccine. But who would Jon alert, who would he tell about it?

Chapter 54

Leon's wife is due to arrive on a bus this evening. *I sense his excitement at seeing her.* This is the longest time they have been apart and he has come to realize how much he misses her. The house is lonely without her and Jon, yet he can't resort to alcohol because of the monitors the Institute installed.

Uncomfortable at the thought of going back to the Extraction Section, that era behind wasn't behind him as he'd thought. Here it is again. I push an image of the woman he last tortured into his mind. He desperately wants a drink. Perhaps he can stop at a bar on the way to pick Barbara up.

He sits alone at a small table in the back corner of a bar is across from the bus depot. *I back off the images.* I don't want him drunk. I feel the burn of the whiskey as it makes its way from his mouth, down his throat and into his stomach.

Leon really doesn't want to start torturing people again. Two drinks later, he walks across the street to meet the arriving bus. In the depot, he greets her. As they hug, he tells her about the bugs in the house, describing where they are located.

"There's probably a bug and a locater beacon in the car too."

They sit on a bench. She looks into his eyes. "Leon, what can we do?"

"I'll go back to the old job. We'll go on as if nothing's changed."

"What about Jon?"

"They really like Jon. I think he's safe as long as he stays at the Institute."

At the house, Leon carries her bags in. He is careful not to give any indication of their knowledge of the cameras.

"You've kept the place pretty clean," comments Barbara.

"I tidied up the garage too. Come have a look."

He shows her the tool cabinet with the removable panel. She looks at the monitors showing her house. She starts to speak. Leon holds his finger to his lips.

"I had Jackson come in every week. He did some nice things to the back yard. I'll show you."

Once outside, Leon leans close to her. "I'm sure there is a bug in the garage, but I found no camera. Anything we have to talk about, we'll do it here, or go out somewhere."

"Leon, we can't live this way."

"It's only temporary until I can figure something out."

* * *

Jon volunteered to give Elena another reading. In her room, he is on the floor, she on the bed. He goes into his trance.

I enter him and Elena. The conduit is established. He sees Elena as energy and all seems quite normal. I tweak Jon to examine her more closely, not looking for problem areas but for abnormalities. He finds the virus, but it seems benign, inert, no more than a curiosity. *At least for now.*

I bring up the image Yoon had on his monitor of the lumpy ball. I will push Jon to study it. I will also inject a feeling to be cautious in his investigation of it.

While I'm in Elena, I tweak the cartoon simulation of her parents' death. I make it a little more realistic. It is still animated characters, but they have features. I feel her jerk back, but she controls her emotions. My plan is to gradually increase the reality. She will have to face it someday. That day is not today.

Jon comes out of his trance. "Are you all right? I felt a shock in you."

"I'm fine. Better than I can remember feeling in quite a while. You look tired. Perhaps it's time for bed."

Jon stands. "These sessions do take some energy out of me. I'll see you tomorrow."

* * *

Yoon stared at the monitor. Through the cam in Elena's room, he had watched the session. The two of them were developing a friendship, maybe more. That was good.

Chapter 55

I'm with Jon and Elena as they are having lunch alone. One of the university students approaches the table.

"Hi, I'm Jill. May I join you?"

They nod and introduce themselves.

Jill smiles. "We are really enjoying the sessions here. The VR system is fascinating. Are you students?"

"We are," answers Jon. "We also work here."

"Oh. What do you do?"

Jon smiles at her. "I do diagnostics. Elena is a surgeon."

Jill's mouth falls open. "That's…that's pretty amazing." She recovers. "We've seen you around and thought you were students. Would you like to come to a little get-together tomorrow evening. It's just us students in the med program here at the Institute."

"We'll have to check schedules. Leave a number and we'll let you know."

Jill writes her number on a napkin. "I hope you can come. See you tomorrow?" She returns to her friends.

"I'd kinda like to go," says Elena. "I haven't been outside of the Institute very much. How about you?"

"Yeah, I'd like to go too. I'll speak to Dr. Yoon."

They glance at the table of students who are huddled together. Once in a while, one would peek at them. No doubt Jill was sharing information that Elena was a surgeon and Jon a diagnostician.

This would be interesting. Would Yoon let them out without chaperons?

* * *

Jon knocked on Yoon's door.

"Come in, Jon."

Jon glanced at the cam mounted above the door as he entered. His father was seated in one of the two chairs in front of the desk. "Your dad and I were just talking about you. How are you doing?"

"I'm fine, sir." Jon paused, then took a breath. "Elena and I were talking to some of the university students. They're having a little get-together tomorrow night and we'd like to go. Would that be all right?"

"The university students?" Yoon glanced at Leon. "I don't see any problem. Do you need a ride?"

"We can take the bus, sir. We won't be late."

"Take good care of yourselves. You both are our star pupils."

"We'll be fine, sir."

Leon turned toward Jon. "You mother is back and would like to see you. Perhaps we can have dinner soon."

"Wow, Mom's back. I'd like to do that. Can we go out for pizza again?" He looked at Yoon, who nodded. "Cool." Jon turned to leave. "I have a reading to do in a few minutes. Thanks. See you tomorrow, Dad."

* * *

Yoon sat and thought for a few minutes. He didn't want the two youths to go out on their own, but he could hardly refuse in front of Jon's father. Perhaps this was a good thing.

Leon would restart the Extraction Program Monday. That was good too. He was still a little concerned about Jon detecting the hidden virus, but at this stage it was inert and harmless. Perhaps it was time for a test. He pulled out the patient list to look for a candidate.

* * *

I'm with Jon and Elena. "We're good to go," says Jon, his enthusiasm apparent in his voice. I sense his anticipation of getting out with other students. Elena is excited too.

Jon's patient is already in the examining room on the table. Jon lies on his table and goes into his trance. I set up the conduit. The woman appears as a mass of energy. Jon begins his examination. She has a tiny lump in her left breast. Jon looks closely.

It's too small to be detected by an x-ray. The color tells Jon it is cancerous. It can be taken out with a small incision. He continues to examine her but sees no other problems. Removal will take care of the situation. He wakes from the trance.

* * *

"Elena, I'll guide you for this operation," says Jon as she looks at his report. "The tumor is in early stages of development, so small you would have trouble finding it."

I am with both Elena and Jon. This will be interesting.

I will try to project Jon's vision into Elena. What Jon sees will be an overlay to what she sees. She will control the robot device completely.

A small incision is made and the laser/probe is inserted. Elena moves it to the spot Jon sees. A quick flash and it is done. The robot sutures the incision.

"We're all done, ma'am. That wasn't so bad, was it?" says Elena.

"I didn't feel anything. You got it all?"

Elena glances at Jon. "Yes, ma'am. No troubles."

They both leave the OR.

They stop in the hall. Elena puts her hand on Jon's arm. "Jon, I could see what you see when you are making a reading. That's amazing. I understand a lot more now. How do you do it?"

"I don't know. It just comes to me."

"Let's get cleaned up and get our party clothes on. I'm ready to see some of the outside world."

"Elena, it would be best if we don't say anything about this, or my readings tonight."

"This is pretty amazing stuff, but you're right. Any revelations should come from Dr. Yoon and the Institute."

Yoon listened to the conversation. He felt his trust in them wasn't misplaced.

Chapter 56

The party is small, only eight people. It is at one of the local bars near campus. Music blares, people are dancing, and the lighting is low. Jon and Elena drink sodas. A pitcher of beer sits beside a large bowl of popcorn on the table in the corner. *I'm in both of them.*

The introductions were made and both Jon and Elena were the object of interest. "How did you end up at the Institute?" asks Jill, looking from Elena to Jon.

Elena speaks first. "I was orphaned and the Institute took me in. I had a knack for medicine. They were developing their teaching system and I was the test subject."

"You're awfully young to be a surgeon," said Bill, one of the students who was in the cafeteria.

"As you know," said Jon, "the Institute's teaching system is radically advanced."

"The robotics are amazing," added Elena. "We feel the definition of surgeon will change in the future from someone who actually performs the surgery to someone who directs it through the robots. Of course, it's all monitored by Dr. Yoon."

Bill's eyes widened as he contemplated this.

"What about you?" asked Jill, turning toward Jon. "You do diagnostics?"

"I do," said Jon. "The computerization allows access to a huge data-base. Put in the right data, and out pops a diagnosis. Then we go check it out."

"We have that here too." said another student. "Putting in the right data and following up with the right tests and examination is the hard part." The others at the table nodded.

"Our database is pretty big, but I'd like to check yours out," said Jon.

And there it is. Jon's opportunity to check out the virus particle he'd found in Elena without oversight. I was proud of myself for pushing that idea into his head.

"We could do that tomorrow," said Jill.

"I don't know what my schedule will be. Can I take a look tonight? It'll only take a few minutes."

"I'll walk him over to the lab," said Bill. "C'mon, Jon. It's close. Won't take long."

"We'll only be a few minutes," said Jon, smiling at Elena.

* * *

The walk takes five minutes. The lab is a room filled with computer terminals. Bill sits at one and logs in. "Here ya go. Have a seat."

Through Jon's eyes, I note the login codes.

Jon sits and places his hands on the keyboard. He types in *virus* as the general topic. He does a search on the Varicella Zoster virus. He turns to Bill. "I'm looking at a patient with Shingles. I'd like to know more."

The picture that comes up is similar to the one he saw in Elena, but with subtle differences. The surface is not as lumpy and the spikes don't have barbs on the ends. He stares at it wondering what the differences will do.

He clicks on the antivirus treatment tab. A list of effective agents is shown. He clicks on one and the picture of the virus shows the changes that happen in the presence of the agent. The lumpy surface cracks, and a substance is exuded. The body's T cells move in identifying the enemy.

The agent makes the virus recognizable as something the body needs to fight. If the agents are not able to do that, the body will not fight the virus.

"This is a pretty cool program," said Jon. "Maybe I can use it more sometime. Let's get back to the party."

Bill logs off and they return to the bar. As they rejoin the group, Elena is describing the robotic surgeon and her directions to it.

"In most cases, the robot is capable of performing the surgery. I act as a monitor. Recently we had a case of a breast tumor so early in the development stage we had to use a special technique."

Under the table, Jon puts his hand on Elena's knee. She glances at him. "It was successful."

"What was the technique?" asks Jill.

"It's one the Institute is developing, so I can't talk about it yet."

Nice save, Elena.

"We need to get back," said Jon. "The last bus leaves in about ten minutes."

He and Elena rise and thank everybody for the invite.

As they stand waiting for the bus, Elena says, "Thanks. I almost opened my mouth. Did you find out anything?"

"They have a good system. We might be able to use it at times. I'll need to compare it to the one at the Institute when we get back."

Chapter 57

I am still a little stunned from my excursion with that vast ocean of knowledge. My mind isn't big enough to take it in. It was overpowering and I had to pull back. The line I followed of Yoon's past extended into the future, or perhaps one possible future if he is allowed to continue. The virus is already inside millions, more likely billions, of people. I did not get the timeline for the release of the activating agent, only that it will happen.

Why do I care? I'm not in that world any more. I have grown to like Jon and certainly Elena. Leon has shown he isn't the cold-blooded torturer I thought. I would hate to see them suffer with uncontrollable Shingles X.

Me caring for people? That's a new revelation. Since I can only interact with the physical world through the minds of people I'm linked to, a sizeable challenge to do anything about this plot awaits.

* * *

I instill fear in Jon that using the Institute's data system to study the Shingles virus could present a danger. He also now suspects the virus he found in Elena was not natural. I push other ideas into his mind, such as it was a modified virus to be used as a weapon. Not knowing who is behind it is his concern. I plant the idea that the Institute had a hand in it. If he searches their database, they will be alerted. He doesn't sleep well.

* * *

I enter Yoon. He received a message approving a test of the virus, the activation agent, and the vaccination. He has chosen Elena as the subject. The activation takes only hours to react.

* * *

"Jon, something's wrong with me. My skin is on fire, a rash has appeared." *They are in Elena's room and I am in them.* She turns her back to him and opens her bathrobe to show him the blisters. "It hurts, a lot. Can you do a reading?"

I'm also with Yoon, who's watching through the CCTV. Elena can't lie down on the bed. Contact with the sheets is too painful. She climbs into the bathtub filled with cool water. Jon lies on the bed. He goes into his trance.

I open the conduit. Elena's energy appears, her form covered in red. Jon goes to the site where the virus was a couple of days before. A swarm of the images flow outward from that site. Millions of them. He knows she has an attack of Shingles X. He withdraws.

"Elena, it's Shingles, a bad case. I'm going to report it to Dr. Yoon. Perhaps he knows of something we can do."

"I'm going to stay here. It's the least painful."

* * *

Distraught, Jon sits in Dr. Yoon's office. "I think Elena has contracted Shingles, and is suffering from an attack. What can we do?"

I'm in both of them.

Yoon wants to wait for a few days to see how bad the attack gets. *Sadistic bastard.*

"Let me look into antivirals to try. We have some here to start with."

He knows they won't work except for the one he developed..

"Thank you, Dr. Yoon." Jon leaves.

* * *

I am going back to the realm of knowledge to see what can be done to thwart this scheme. Again, I reach out and am taken into this dimension. I pull back before I am in too deep, but maintain the contact. Information about this virus flows. Much of it I don't understand. I do learn the Shingles virus resides in anyone who has had chicken pox. Dr. Yoon's virus is different. It has been manipulated to specifically attack the spinal nerves and resist the Shingrix vaccine.

Is it possible to tweak Shingrix to work against this virus? I check and see that it is. I have the information. I can give it to Jon along with a strong caution. But then what can he do with it? If Yoon finds out he's looking into a vaccine to his virus, Jon and his family will disappear.

* * *

Jon and I are with Elena. She is still in pain, but the cool soak has helped. She is still in the tub.

Jon taps on the bathroom door.

"It's okay. Come on in," says Elena as she pulls a towel into the tub, covering herself.

Jon enters and closes the door.

"What did you see in your reading?"

Jon goes to the Institute intercom and puts on some music. "The affected area was red, like a hot spot. I looked closely and saw the actual virus. It is different from the one I saw in the data-base at the university. Something changed."

"Has it morphed?"

I give Jon a push. "That, or it was created."

Surprise shows on her face. "Who would do that?"

"An enemy."

She stares at him. "Can it be treated?"

I bring up the information I got along with an idea to use the university database to look.

"I'm going to use the university system to do a little search."

Elena looks at him. "Why not use the one here?"

"I like that one better." Jon glances at the closed door.

Elena watches him. "Is there a problem here?"

Jon shrugs. "I don't know. I'll get over there as soon as I can. I have a reading to do and I'll be back." He leaves.

* * *

Two hours later, he returns. "How are you doing?"

Elena is in her bathrobe sitting on the bed. "The soak helped, but I'm getting back in the tub soon."

There is a soft knock at Elena's door. "Come in."

Dr. Yoon enters. "Jon told me about your condition. How are you doing?"

"The pain is still pretty bad, but the soak helped."

Yoon nods. "I have done some research and found a vaccine that seems promising." He takes out a syringe. Jon watches him.

"If it will help, I want it," says Elena.

Yoon injects her. "I'll check back with you in twelve hours to see if there's any change." He leaves.

"I guess you won't have to go to the database at the uni," says Elena.

"I still want to. I'm having dinner with my parents tomorrow night. Perhaps I can do it then."

Chapter 58

I am with Yoon and Kwang. Entering two or more people at the same time has become easier. Practice, I guess. Yoon is bringing Kwang up to date on the plan.

"I have infected the girl Elena with the Shingles X virus. The symptoms were severe and progressed faster than anticipated. I have since injected her with our vaccine to see how effective it is."

"Our factory awaits proof of the vaccine's efficacy before they begin production," said Kwang. "We are perhaps days away from the PRK path to becoming a world power."

* * *

Not if I can help it. I have the formula for the vaccine but how do I publish it? That has to be through Jon. I create a dream in him.

* * *

I enter Jon and Leon. The family is at the pizza place with kids running amok. Leon recognizes the man who entered his house sitting by himself at another table. They are still tailing him.

He leans close to Jon. "Don't look now, but the man in the corner is the one who has been following us. He can't hear what we say with all the kids." Jon casually glances around the room as if checking out the pandemonium. "The Institute wants me to restart the Extraction program," says Leon. "I really don't want to do it. If I refuse, he," Leon nods at the man, "will probably pay us a visit." Jon resists the urge to look at the man.

Leon's wife says nothing, but she is alert to every word. She glances at the man in the corner. "Should we take care of him?" Both Leon and Jon look at her in surprise. "You don't think I'm going to let my family be killed, do you?"

"You never say anything," says Leon. "And now you come out with this?"

"I talked things over with my sister. She never let anybody run over her, even in the Marines. One call to her, and she'll be here to help."

"If we do anything to him, we will have to leave immediately afterward."

"Maybe yes, maybe no," says Barbara.

"Dad, I need to go the medical library at the university for a while. I think worse things than the Extraction program are going on."

I bring up the information about the Shingles X virus and the vaccine Jon had dreamt of.

Jon leans close to his father. "I think Yoon and Kwang are enemy agents of some kind. Something is planned, an attack with a bio agent."

Leon stares at Jon as if he's lost his mind. Jon hurries on. "Elena came down with a Shingles attack. It was horrible. Yoon injected her with a vaccine he said he found, but I think there's more to it."

"How do you get from that to them being agents? That's quite a leap."

Jon leans close to his mother and father. "I know it sounds crazy. I had a strange dream, not a nightmare like the others."

"I haven't had the nightmares for a while," said Leon.

"Me neither," said Jon. "I did a reading on Elena and the Shingles virus. I was able to see the actual virus." His mother looks puzzled. Jon explains. "I do these readings on people. I'm able to see what's going on with them physically and it allows me to diagnose their problems."

"What!" says Barbara, a puzzled look on her face. "How do you do that?"

"I go into some kind of trance and examine the patient. I don't see just the physical body but I see the energies that surround it, actually make it up. I can see the disparities, the problems that throw it out of balance."

His mother looks stunned. She doesn't understand.

"It's why the Institute likes me. I've helped them treat patients."

"How does this happen?" asked Barbara.

"I don't know." I discovered this ability during the virtual reality lessons. At first, Yoon didn't believe I could diagnose this way. It was too accurate to deny."

"You can do this with anybody?" she asks.

"I think so."

"Your nightmares stopped but you still dream?" Leon asks.

"I dream now, but yeah, the nightmares have stopped."

"Mine too, but that's one thing that worries me about starting the Extraction program again."

Jon nods, understanding how that could happen. "How do we lose the tail?"

"We'll go back to the house. They watch it with hidden cameras and mics, but I can take care of those. You can catch the bus from there to the university."

As they leave, the man in the corner follows. At the house, Leon shows Jon the panel. He writes on a pad, *No camera in here, I think, but there is a microphone. You claim to be tired and want to lie down for a while. I'll loop you sleeping. You can slip out.*

Jon nods. They sit at the kitchen table talking a while before Jon says he wants a short nap.

* * *

At the university, Jon walks into the medical library and sits at one of the stations. He closes his eyes. *I project the login procedure.* Now what? he thinks.

I project the information about the virus and the modification to the Shingrix vaccine that is effective against it into Jon.

He goes onto the Wiki site and starts a new topic titled: **An innovative Shingles vaccine.** He enters everything I transfer into him including the new Shingles X virus and the way to modify the Shingrix vaccine to treat it. When he logs off, he notices an hour has passed. Time to get back to the house. He texts his dad: OMW.

As he enters the house through the back door, he gives them a thumbs up. His dad points to the bedroom. Ten minutes later his dad knocks on his bedroom door.

"You probably need to get back to the Institute. It's getting late. The last bus is in fifteen minutes."

They hug at the door. "We need to get together more often," says Leon.

"How about in a week?" asks Jon.

* * *

Yoon meets Jon at the door. "How was your evening?"

"It was great to see my mom again. She hasn't seen her sister in years, so it was a kind of a reunion for her. I met my aunt once but I was really young and don't remember her at all." He yawns. "With all that's been happening with Elena and the readings, I'm pretty tired. I took a short nap–in my own bed. I liked it."

Yoon smiled. "Well, get some rest. We have several patients lined up for you tomorrow. Maybe you can take a reading on Elena to see if the vaccine has been effective."

"I'm going to read up on Shingles," says Jon. "Is there much in our database?"

"Information is available."

"I don't know how much I'll get to tonight." Jon yawns again. "I'd like to see if Elena's better." He turns toward his room. "Thank you, sir. I'll see you in the morning.

I read a little suspicion in Yoon, but it's nothing he can put his finger on.

Chapter 59

I set up the conduit from the dimension of knowledge to Jon for his readings. It's becoming a familiar routine. Elena's body energy is much more balanced. The vaccine is working and I feel Jon's is relief. Yoon is watching, and I sense his satisfaction at the success of the vaccine. The plan is unfolding.

* * *

I am in Yoon. That satisfaction is short-lived when he receives a message from the People's Republic of Korea. All it says is: *check out the Wiki article.* With a feeling of trepidation, he logs onto his computer and the site. Under his search for Shingles, the article pops up. As he reads, he is stunned, then his stomach knots. The description is exactly how the virus was developed and how the vaccine was created. Who put this on here?

Obviously, there is a leak. He texts back to the PRK: Leak on your end? No one here knows of this.

The reply says: Investigating.

He knows what that means and is glad he's not there.

He stands and paces in his office. The information on that site is now public information. His lab could claim precedence and try for a patent. They have the records showing the PRK lab was first to develop it, but that would open up the whole scheme. He shakes his head. It may come out anyway. That the Shingles X virus was created could be determined and might be traced back to his lab.

Yoon leans on his desk. Look at the mess that COVID 19 created for the Wuhan Institute of Virology. It cost the Chinese government millions to show it didn't originate there but was from animals.

Yoon calls Kwang. "We have problems."

* * *

Kwang was stunned at the news. "When did you find out?"

"I just got a text an hour ago. They only text in an emergency."

"How could this have happened?"

"Obviously, there is a leak. With all the detail, it has to be in Korea. Nobody here knows anything about my background or the development of Shingles X. There is nothing in the files. They are investigating now. Heads will roll, some innocent, others not."

Kwang is frozen. "Let me see the post on Wiki."

Yoon boots up his computer and navigates to the site and the article.

Kwang reads it, then reads it again. "Look at the posting date!" He turns to Yoon while pointing at the screen. "It went up last night."

I try to suppress the niggling thought in Yoon that somehow Jon had anything to do with it. He checks the logons at the Institute for anything about Shingles X or a vaccine. Nothing. Jon was gone last night. The monitor on Leon's computer also came up negative. No activity last night.

This is silly. Jon couldn't have anything to do with this leak. Still, he reviews the CCTV recordings of Leon's house from last night. It is as Jon said, he took a nap and only left the house to return to the Institute. Dr. Yoon checks Jon's online activity. He did look into the database and read about the Shingles virus this morning. There was no other activity. He did not go to the Wiki site.

He tries to dismiss his uneasiness. Jon has no way of knowing any of the information. *Unless his reading ability has expanded.* Yoon shakes his head.

I project: *That's not possible.*

Yoon's phone signals he has received another text. It is Korea. As he reads, the disturbing news creates anger and fear. The whole program is compromised. With the public knowledge of a vaccine that will work against Shingles X, anybody can manufacture it. The only advantage is the Korean manufacture can start immediately. He texts back: *Test of vaccine successful. Do not release activation chemical. Start manufacture of vaccine immediately. We will market the vaccine as a replacement for Shingrix, one more permanent and more effective. Use documentation of development with dates to apply for patent.* He hits send.

At least the program is not a complete loss.

* * *

He turns on the monitor showing Jon in a trance doing a reading. He watches.

How does he do it?

Chapter 60

All of the mental activity has exhausted me. While drifting in my realm, I can feel the attraction of the dimension of knowledge trying to pull me in. That draw comes from within me, but I resist. I'm not ready to stop being me. Every time I enter that realm, the lure to stay in Paradise grows stronger. For most of the souls here, this is hell, but not for me. I do not long for the physical world I cannot remember, nor am. I tied to the temptations of objects, power, or status. Concerns with what happens to the other souls here do not bother me. They arrive, they stay or they go.

I do wish revenge against the Institute and their torturous program. I do want to stop the program to activate a virus that would cause millions great pain. Perhaps that does tie me to the physical world. I could merge with the dimension of knowledge and realize what I have to do for that. Eventually, I will not be able to resist it. I long for it.

* * *

I enter Yoon. His concern about the leak is growing. He has heard nothing for the last two weeks from the PRK. They have not found the source. The disclosure of the virus and the vaccine has destroyed years of planning.

In any investigation, the origin of Shingles X will be determined as artificial. If it is tied to North Korea, world condemnation will follow. Everybody associated with this project will disappear. He covers his face with his hands. What a reversal! Now they must guard against the release of the activating agent.

* * *

He and Kwang have been talking to the university about a merger. The technology created by the Institute is better than anything else in use today. The students who have attended sessions at the Institute have accelerated in their learning and the university is open to a relationship. A merger would open the university data-base for the Institute. And a ready marketing program for their technology. That's the good news.

The last message from the PRK indicated the IP address for whoever posted the information about Shingles X and the vaccine on Wiki was from a university computer. He has no idea how that information could have gotten to them, but with an arrangement he could investigate.

* * *

Leon has moved back into the Extraction program. The separation of any empathy for the subjects and the pain he inflicts is not as easy to maintain as it once was. He hates this job.

I have not interrupted his sleep with nightmares as I did before. If his performance suffers, his life and that of his wife could be in danger. I hesitate to be with him during the torture sessions. The painful memories are all I have of my physical existence. Still, he does have sleeping problems, and the images of the subjects' suffering at his hands haunt him.

In the morning before leaving for work, he checks the recordings of the bugs planted in his home by the Institute looking for any hint they are dissatisfied. After catching glimpses of the man who followed his family, he knows he is still being watched. With a shudder, he boards the bus for work. His only bright spot is that he and Jon are having dinner tonight.

* * *

The pizza restaurant is filled with children celebrating a birthday. Kids are running around yelling. The token operated game machines are flashing and ringing. Leon's shadow sits alone at a corner table.

"What have you found out?" asks Leon, leaning toward Jon.

Jon straightens up and looks at the kids as if showing mild interest in the joyful pandemonium. "I posted information about the virus and the vaccine on the Wiki site." His voice is soft and sure not to carry beyond their table. "It's now public domain and anybody can manufacture the vaccine. That'll piss them off."

"More than that," says Leon. "Years of work went into this scheme. Heads will roll. They won't stop until they find the source."

"I was careful, Dad."

Leon laughed. "Let's celebrate."

Their pizza is delivered.

Chapter 61

Kwang and Yoon presented a plan to form a merger with the university. The Institute would become a satellite medical campus. The advanced medical techniques and equipment from the Institute would be a welcome addition to the medical school, and the resources of the university would be helpful to the Institute.

After approval by his bosses on the PRK to move ahead with the merger, it is fast-tracked with an expanded lease arrangement of Institute facilities for a nominal fee. With access to the university databases, Yoon looked at the login record starting the day before the Wiki posting occurred. Many students had logged in over the two days before it showed up. But only Bill Jacobs, a third-year med student, had logged in the night before. He went to the Wiki site.

Yoon stared at the screen. Perhaps he needed a chat with Bill. The students were having a session at the Institute later today. Bill would be there.

* * *

I am with Dr. Yoon as he walks into the cafeteria. The more I am with him, the better I get at inserting thoughts in his mind. He quickly spots the university students at a table with Jon and Elena. As he walks up, they all look at him.

"I'm sure you remember me from our introduction at the first of the term, but I am Dr. Yoon, Medical Supervisor at the Institute." He held out his hand to the first student on his right.

"I'm Natalie Johnson," she said, shaking the offered hand.

He continues with each student. "We have been working with the university to make the Institute a partner. It will mean additional classes and more of our technology will be available." He smiles. "We're still working on a curriculum that will include more advanced use of our VR tools. As a part of that, I'd like to sit down with each of you one-on-one to get your impressions, ideas and suggestions. Perhaps we could start this afternoon."

The students nod. To have the opportunity to give input was something they were not used to.

* * *

As part of these discussions, the students sign Non-Disclosure Agreements. The merger deal with the university did not include the rights to the technology…yet. The interviews are routine. The students mostly expressing the approval of the VR system in glowing terms. Several students put forth ideas to expand the teaching to include the robot surgery sessions with Elena.

One of those is Bill Jacobs. Yoon hands him the NDA. "This is to protect our technology until something is worked out with the university. No publishing or discussions are allowed." He watches Bill closely for any reaction as he reads over it.

Bill shrugs. "We have those with the U for stuff. No big deal." He signs.

Yoon sees nothing to indicate Bill had posted anything. Is he a good actor? If he didn't do it, who did? The login at the time of the Wiki posting was with his credentials. Was it possible someone else had used his password? Who? More critically, how did whoever posted get the information?

"You must be quite a dedicated student," says Yoon. "I want to thank you for socializing with Jon and Elena. They don't get out much, certainly not into the expanded availability offered by the university database. What do you think of them?"

Bill smiles. "They're both quite young to be as advanced as they are. They illustrate the value of the technology of this Institute. Elena's experience with the robotic surgery is way beyond anything we have. I'm most anxious to observe her in the OR."

Yoon nods. "She's been working at it for a while. Her experience has helped us develop improvements. What do you think about Jon and his diagnostics?"

"We have good diagnostic tools, but as Jon says, the input is everything. I'm sure his experience in assessing the computer results is valuable."

I feel Yoon's relief that nothing about Jon's ability and his readings was discussed. He will have to share that with the university eventually, but narrowly revealed to only a few people and when the time seems right.

"Jon showed some interest in our data system," Bill continues. "I took him over to the lab and showed him how it works. Is he interested in viruses?"

Yoon froze for a second. "We had a case of Shingles occur here recently."

"He did look at some information about Shingles. He felt the university system might have more up-to-date material. "We were only logged on for a few minutes, not long enough to do any assessment."

Yoon stands. "Bill, Thank you for your input. I look forward to having you and other students here." He shakes Bill's hand.

* * *

I plant a question in Yoon's mind. Could someone in the PRK lab have spoofed the IP address?

Yoon writes down a list of the people he worked with while there. He had been ambitious and driven. A number of people resented his success and might take any opportunity to strike at him. He puts check marks next to those names.

I hope that is enough of a red herring to keep Jon off the suspect list.

Chapter 62

I am with Jon and Elena as they eat dinner. Both are tired. Elena performed several surgeries, and Jon did four readings.

Dr. Yoon sits down with them. "Elena, how are you feeling?"

"I'm fine, though not as energetic as I was before the Shingles outbreak."

"It can take a little time to get over that. Don't get overly tired or stressed. It could reoccur, and we don't want a setback."

"I know I don't," she says. "That was one of the worst experiences I've ever had."

Yoon looks at Jon. You're looking tired also. Are you okay?"

"For some reason I had to focus much harder today. I don't know why. It was much more tiring than in the past."

I had established the connection with the realm of knowledge, but didn't push the data as much as in the past. I want to see if Jon can pull it out and eventually be able to do his readings without me.

"Jon, when you came to me with the diagnosis of Shingles in Elena, what did you see?"

I set off an alarm in Jon's head. Be careful.

"Usually, I see the energy surrounding a person. Different levels are different systems. They are balanced in a healthy person. Changes in the balance indicate problems. What I saw in Elena was a red glow, but within her and around her spine. Threads from it extended out into her body. I'm not sure why I thought of Shingles. I hadn't studied it before. The word just popped into my head. That's when I came to see you."

"I'm glad you did. Have you studied it since?"

"I have. I looked it up in our system, and when Elena and I were at the university for the little party, I looked it up on their database. The information seemed to be the same."

Yoon smiles. "I'm glad you took the initiative to research it. I've always felt our database was up to date, but I feel more certain now."

He glances from Jon to Elena. "As you may know, we are in discussion with the university to partner with them. They have approved starting more advanced programs. Tomorrow, some of them are going to observe your surgery, Elena."

He turns to Jon. "I'd like to have them observe you, but I'm not sure what there is to see."

Jon laughs. "Watching me stretched out on a table wouldn't be too exciting."

Yoon rises. "Get some rest. See you tomorrow."

Jon can see that Elena is nervous. "Don't worry. Just ignore them and do what you usually do. Afterward, show the video and take questions."

"They already have robots doing surgery at the U. I'm not sure ours will impress them."

"You're not trying to impress them, so don't worry about it. What's unique with you is the intimate knowledge of the robots. At other robot ERs, a rep from the manufacturer is present, but you have supplanted that need."

* * *

In his room, Yoon paces and reviews his conversation with Jon about his search for information about Shingles. His phone sounds. It is Kwang.

"I've been recalled to the PRK for an interview." His voice is shaky.

Yoon sits. "When do you leave?"

"Tomorrow. You will have to fill in for me. The liaison from the university has an appointment with me at ten-o'clock. You will have to take that meeting. Have her sign the NDA and take her on a tour through the facilities. I believe she will be most interested in the VR section."

"Do you have any indication why you have to return to the PRK?"

"They didn't say, but we both know it has to do with the leak of information about Shingles X and the vaccine."

Both Yoon and Kwang are worried. Shoot first and ask question later has always been the policy with this administration.

"Be careful," says Yoon. "You'll be okay. I've been doing my own investigation here, and I'm sure nobody has the knowledge to create that post."

"I hope that's enough," says Kwang.

"I'll take care of things until you return." *IF you return*, he thinks.

* * *

Dr. Patricia Victory sat in Yoon's office. She was a short woman, a bit stocky with shoulder-length gray hair. She would be the main contact between the Institute and the university under their new arrangement.

"Dr. Victory, have you seen our facility before?" asked Yoon.

"Patricia, please. My predecessor got your tour. He retired two months ago and I'm just now getting my feet on the ground." She smiled. "My students have high praise for your program."

Yoon passed her the NDA form. She read it quickly.

"A standard form. We have one quite similar we'll be sending over to you." She signed it. "Hopefully, our legal departments will quickly come up with an arrangement where we can freely share what we have."

* * *

The first stop was the Virtual Reality lab. Yoon had her don the VR headset and put her through the intro to anatomy.

"I can see why the students like this," Patricia said as she removed the headset. "This is way beyond anything we have. How many students can you handle at a time?"

"This is a one-at-a-time setup. With additional funding, we would like to expand it so that ten students can have individual experiences simultaneously."

"That is one place we can help. We have funds available."

Yoon laughed. "That would be most helpful. If you would put the headset back on, we can observe a surgery taking place at the moment."

Patricia was virtually in the OR with Elena, the only human in the operating room other than the patient. On the table was a young woman.

I am with Elena and Yoon. "I want you to count backward from one-hundred," says Elena as she watches the monitors. At ninety-one, the woman's eyes close. A hologram shows a tube as it being fed into her carotid artery through a small incision. A glowing red section on the monitor is the location of a tumor. On the hologram, a thin fiber from the tube emits a laser beam.

A different monitor shows the view from the tube. The laser begins to cut away the dark section. Another tube sucks the cuttings away while a third has arms that pull the cut sections together where the laser fuses the cut edges. Elena watches, ready to do take over if something isn't right.

"That's amazing," said Patricia, removing the headset. "I've never seen anything like that."

"It's all done robotically," says Yoon. "Once we outline the tumor, it automatically performs the surgery. We'll monitor her. That's why the NDA. We'll apply for patents next month."

"The tumor was quite small. How did you diagnose it at such an early stage?"

Yoon leads her back to his office.

I can feel his unease about revealing information about Jon, but it will have to come out.

"What you are about to see is something we don't fully understand. We would like you to keep this to yourself at this time." He turns on a wall monitor. She sees at a young man lying on a table, his eyes closed. In an adjacent room is another man on a table.

"What am I seeing?" she asks.

"The boy is doing a remote reading on the man. He will diagnose the problem. Sometimes it requires surgery, sometimes medication will cure him. Sometimes a holistic approach will work."

"I don't understand."

"To be honest, neither do I," said Yoon. "His accuracy in diagnosis is nearly one-hundred-percent. We have verified it."

Dr. Victory shook her head. "There's no way to duplicate that, is there?"

"Sadly, not that we've found. Jon is the object of study for us."

"Have you done an MRI or an EEG while he's in that state?"

"We're very careful to not disturb whatever's there." Yoon looked at her sharply. "It's the goose and golden egg thing. We restrict who gets to see this. I'm trusting you. Less than ten people know about Jon. The last thing we want is a parade of people coming through or some press agent speaking of voodoo medicine. All we know at this point is it works."

They watch as Jon dictates the condition: Testicular cancer. Early stages. Surgery is warranted.

Chapter 63

I am with Jon and Elena. "How did your surgery go today," asks Jon. They are at dinner in the cafeteria.

"I didn't even know anybody was there. They watched both of them on VR."

"Did they have questions?"

"Oh yeah. I answered most of them. Some were too detailed and technical about the robots. I didn't have the answers. It made me realize there's more to learn. I told them my confidence in the system was extremely high."

"Elena, despite what they think, you are the surgeon. The robots are only machines."

She gave him a weak thank you smile. "They also wanted to know how we were able to detect the tumor and the cancer at such an early phase. I said it was our diagnostician who alerted us."

Jon groaned. "They'll be coming after me next. I have no answers as to how or why."

Elena smiles. "How did your readings go?"

Jon frowns. "It was harder than in the past. Before, the energy fields surrounding the body just appeared. Today, I had to focus and try to pull the vision together. It wore me out."

Elena put her hand on Jon's arm. "What you do is like a miracle, you know."

"What's the old saying? 'When people don't understand the science, it's a miracle.' Or something like that. I don't understand the science."

"How are you going to answer their questions?"

"I don't know." He laughed. "That will be my answer."

* * *

I am in Yoon and he is listening to Jon and Elena. Perhaps he had erred in showing Dr. Victory Jon's reading. Today has been an epic day for revealing secrets. He tried to call Kwang. No answer. He glanced at the clock. The flight should have landed two hours ago.

The stress of what's happening has softened the lock Yoon keeps on his mind. *I now have the key and am able to get in. I insert a little worry worm in his mind. Tonight, nightmares await.*

* * *

The pull of the realm of knowledge on me grows stronger. The more I use it the harder it is for me to resist. Two things prevent me from joining. The other souls here are tied to the physical world and that holds them back. I realize I am too, with this need for revenge and the desire to help Jon, Elena, and Leon. I recognize them as the chains they are to me. And I don't mind.

The other thing holding me back is my resistance to release my identity, my ego, and become one with the dimension of knowledge. Every time I am with it, I realize what a wonderful place it is. But I still want my individuality. Or perhaps I'm afraid of giving it up.

My test to see if Jon is able to perform readings without my help shows he is not quite ready. He is able to hold the connection, but it takes great effort. I will continue assisting but at a decreasing level. I feel confident he is capable. I now see this as preparation for my departure from this realm.

I check on Kwang. He is in a cell awaiting questioning about the failure of the Shingles X project to move forward. I do believe that questioning will be very similar to the work Leon does in the Extraction section. There will be questions he has no answers to, but that won't stop the questioning. No pity from me. There will be no going back to the Institute.

I enter the dreams of Yoon. His sleep is troubled. I project an image of Kwang under torture accusing Yoon of posting the ruinous information on Wiki. He hears the stamp of jackboots outside his room and the thunder of pounding on his door. He awakes with a scream. Sweat soaks the sheets. His heart is running away, trying to escape from his chest. He looks around wildly. The dream is slow to fade.

The ritual of making tea calms him. If he is taken back to the PRK, someone has to take over the Institute. He wants it to continue. Instead of a merger, perhaps the university would be interested in taking over it as a satellite campus. As administrator, Dr. Victory will play a much larger part than she imagined.

He has to tidy things up.

The Extraction Program has to be erased. It was very promising. If they'd only had a few more months…. The records will have to be scrubbed of all reference to human extraction. The chambers in the basement will have to be sanitized and turned into storage rooms. And Leon. That loose end needs to be dealt with.

Yoon is not able to take out Jon. He is too precious, and now too many people know about him. He forms a list in his mind of tasks he cannot write down. As the sun comes up, he calls Eric Rumbel.

"It's Yoon," he says to the sleep-filled voice on the other end of the phone. "Time to tidy up the Proskys. I'll keep Jon here, but Leon and his wife need to go. Make it look like an accident. Use as many people as you think necessary."

"Got it, Boss." The line was already dead.

Chapter 64

I warn Leon. He has the most vivid dream he's had in months. A black shadow is creeping toward his house. Evil descends like a blanket. He knows what it means. He wakes Barbara.

"Call your sister. Take the bus to the motel and truck stop on the east side of town with your go bag."

She is instantly awake. "What are you going to do?"

"I'm going to work as if nothing is happening. Today, rather than take the bus, I'll drive. I'll figure it out from there. I have remote access to the security cams in our house, so I can check on it. I'll meet you at the motel after work and we'll put together a plan.

I'm going to stay with Leon.

As he checks in through security at the Institute a message appears on his phone: Go to Supervisor Yoon's office. In the elevator he calms himself. *They wouldn't try anything here,* he thinks as he exits the elevator.

Leon glances up at the camera mounted above Yoon's door. He knocks.

"Come in, Leon."

Yoon is sitting behind his desk and gestures Leon to a chair. "Have a seat." Yoon's smile seems strained. Leon notices Yoon shows tension in his face and his posture. Something is wrong.

"As you may know things at the Institute will be changing. We are going to join in a partnership with the university. We'll approach them about creating a satellite campus out of the Institute. They will be in charge."

This news stuns Leon. "What about Dr. Kwang and you?"

"Dr. Kwang will not be returning. He has taken another position overseas. I may be joining him. Dr. Patricia Victory will be the new administrator. She will need cooperation from everybody for this to go smoothly."

"And the Extraction Program?"

We will have to shut that down and clean everything up. I don't want any traces left."

"I'm glad sir. I was struggling with it. I'm sure it shows in my results."

Yoon holds up his hand. "Leon, it's okay. We'll put you back in the maintenance section. I just wanted you to know. I understand this is a lot to swallow, but it came on very fast for me too. Why don't you take the day off. Go home and spend some time with your wife. Take her out to dinner on the company.

"That's very generous, sir. Thank you."

"I'll have lunch with you and Jon tomorrow. When you arrive in the morning, clean up the chambers in the basement. We want no trace of that program to be misinterpreted by our new partners." Yoon rises, signaling the meeting is over.

Leon goes out to his car. He drives a block away to a shopping center parking lot and removes the tracker and bug and puts them in a copper box. With the car clean he texts Barbara: *Got the day off. On my way home. Get ready for a fun day.* He texts Jon: *Plan B.* He pulls the sim card from his phone, inserts another.

At the motel, Barbara stares at his face. "What's wrong?"

"The hit is on."

"I called my sister, Ginger. I left no message. The call is the signal. She'll be coming in on the four-thirty flight and look for me."

"Good. I'll go to the storage yard and pick up some equipment. Be back here in a couple of hours."

On the way to Extra Closet Storage, he stops at the carwash and gas station. At the storage yard, he keys in the code and enters. Leon drives into the large storage garage and rolls down the door. He loads the trunk and back seat with guns, ammo, and the provisions for a trip. Next, he masks off the chrome, lights, and windows on the car, dons a respirator and opens up a case of spray paint. Within an hour, the dull white car is a dark gray sedan. Not a good job, but different enough to throw off the casual observer. He changes the license plate to one from out of state.

Back at the motel, Leon pulls up the video from his home system on his new laptop. Three men wearing masks and carrying rifles enter his house. He watches as they clear the house, then make themselves comfortable. They could have a long wait, he thinks. *The longer the better.* He watches as the man who had been following him uses his cellphone. The microphone picks up him speaking.

"Nobody here." There's a pause. "The tracker signal has dropped out. Either he found it or the thing quit working." Another pause. "We'll wait here until they come back."

* * *

At the airport, he drops his wife off and parks in the cell phone waiting lot. He texts Jon on his second phone: *We're at the motel with provisions. You're valuable to the Institute, so you'll be safe*

there. It's me they're after. Will call you tonight.
He gets a text. Barbara and Ginger are waiting.

I read Leon's feelings about Barbara's sister.
Ginger had not been in their lives much. She was
ex-military and had traveled a lot. Her sandy-
blond hair was short, cut just below her ears. She
was moderate height and looked fit. Years ago,
when Leon asked her about what she did, she gave
him a faint smile. "I can't tell you. It's classified."

At the motel he brings up the cameras from
the house.

Ginger looks over his shoulder. "Three of
them. What do you want to do?"

"Let them sit overnight," says Leon.
"Tomorrow we can call in a wellness check to the
cops."

"They'll still be out there." Ginger shakes her
head. "And they'll know you're onto them."

"By tomorrow they'll know that anyway.
What do you suggest?"

"You have a drone?"

Leon nods. "It's a toy I gave Jon for
Christmas a year ago."

"Let's look for their car."

* * *

At the little park a block from his house, Leon launches the small drone. Starting at his house, he flies a search pattern. The empty house for sale on the next block has a car in the drive. "I've seen that black car before on the trip back from Albuquerque," he says, pointing. "Okay, now what?"

Ginger opens a small box from her luggage and takes out what appears to be a two barreled epoxy syringe. She puts it in a shoulder bag. "Stay here."

With the drone, they see her walk to the car. She glances around to make sure nobody is watching. The street is deserted. Within seconds, she's inside. The tint on the windows is too dark to see what she's doing. A few minutes later she gets out, takes off a gasmask, gloves and plastic coat, and puts them in a heavy-duty plastic bag. She walks to the back of the black car and places something under the bumper. Popping the trunk, she puts the bag inside.

"What did you do?" asks Leon as she opens the passenger door and gets in behind Barbara.

"I left a little present for them."

"Present?" asks Barbara.

"They won't be a problem any longer. You have their tracker?"

Leon holds up the copper box.

"Let's put that on another car."

Behind the motel, Leon puts the tracker on an idling semi. In the growing gloom of night, nobody sees him.

Back in the room, they watch as the man who'd been following them calls from Leon's house.

"The tracker came back up. It's on the highway moving east. We're going to follow it out of town and intercept. A car crash would be a good accident." He hangs up and they leave.

"What's going to happen now?" asks Leon.

"They're going to have a fatal accident. The fire will destroy them and the evidence."

"How do you know this?" asks Barbara.

"There's VX on the steering wheel and on the seats. Without injections of atropine, it's fatal. I doubt they have any in the car. The fire will destroy any residual agent."

"What's VX?" asks Barbara.

"It's a chemical nerve agent," answers Ginger. "It's supposed to be outlawed throughout the world, but the Russians always cheat. Sadam Hussain used it on the Kurds. Killed a lot of people."

"How did you get it?" asks Leon.

"It's not that tough to make. Let's follow them to be sure."

"You don't fuck around, do you," says Leon.

"Not when my baby sister is at risk."

"I thought you had a desk job in the Marines," says Barbara.

"Yeah, that was the cover story. If I told you what I did, I'd have…"

"Say no more," says Leon.

Chapter 65

Dr. Yoon sits with Jon and Elena having dinner in the cafeteria. He is waiting for the call his team has completed their task with Jon's parents. He had expected to hear something an hour ago when he was in his office. Nothing. He would call them after dinner.

"Jon, yesterday you struggled in your readings. Is it better today?"

I am with them. Jon looks at Dr. Yoon, who doesn't look good. His eyes are puffy and red, and the lines around them seem deeper. "Dr. Yoon, are you all right? You look tired."

"I didn't sleep well. Handling my job and Dr. Kwang's is stressful, especially with this deal with the university taking place.

"Deal with the university?" asks Elena.

"The university wants the Institute to become a satellite campus. We're working on a deal now. It's moving very fast."

"The Institute will become part of the university?" asks Jon.

"That is the plan. Dr. Kwang has already accepted a position at another facility." He shrugs. "I may join him."

"It will seem so strange here without you," said Elena.

"Thank you for saying that. Whatever happens, I will be fine."

Not if I can help it. I plan to intensify the images tonight.

"Dr. Yoon, you asked about my readings this morning. They were easier than yesterday, but still required more effort than in the past. I'm not sure what's happening, but I'm still able to do them."

Yoon nods and turns to Elena. "You look recovered from your bout with Shingles. Are you fine?"

"I am. My surgeries today went quite well. I feel like I'm back to my old self."

"Good. I want to let you both know there will be additional visitors from the university. Please show them every courtesy." He stands. "I need to get back to my office."

In his office, I can feel Yoon's concern as he dials the number for Eric Rumbel, his asset and assassin. The call goes straight to voicemail. "Damn!" he exclaims out loud as he stops himself from throwing the phone. Perhaps they're in some critical action and turned their phones off, he thinks.

Or maybe something has gone horribly wrong, I plant in his mind.

* * *

From several car lengths back, Leon keeps black car in view. It is trailing the semi using it as a screen from what they think is Leon's car in front. This section of the interstate is straight and traffic is light, but ahead is a pass through some low mountains. On Leon's laptop, they watch as the tracker signal from the truck is moving just below the speed limit.

Ginger glances at her watch. "The pass would be a good area for an accident. They should start to figure out your car isn't in front of the semi. It won't matter, the VX is going to kick in about now."

The black car speeds up to pass the semi, but then swerves before straightening out and dropping back behind the truck. For the next couple of miles, it weaves, as it follows the semi. Entering the pass, the road has a series of curves. Pulling out again to pass, it swerves badly, then overcorrects. It slues sideways, skids, hits a guardrail, and launches into the air. It lands upside down in a ditch.

Leon pulls off along with several other cars. A cloud of dust hangs in the air. People run toward the car. Ginger hits a button on a remote, and a small explosion near the gas tank drives back the would-be rescuers. Flames appear. The crowd moves farther away. With a whomp, a ball of fire shoots up as the gas tank ignites. A black cloud of smoke builds and rises into the air.

"Nothing we can do here," says Ginger. "Let's go home."

They cross over the median and head back to town. Several miles down the road, emergency vehicles with lights flashing and sirens wailing pass them.

* * *

It's early morning in North Korea. Yoon is frantic he hasn't heard from Rumbel. He tries to call Kwang again. Voicemail. He leaves a message to call him back. As a last resort, he calls the one friend he had at the lab.

"Ahn, this is Yoon. How are you?"

"Dr. Yoon. I haven't heard from you in quite a while. A lot happening here. Many people are being questioned about your project."

"Anything come out of that?" Yoon can hear the nervousness in his own voice.

"I don't know. They have not returned."

"Dr. Kwang was to be there to help. Have you seen him?"

"No. I must go." The line went dead.

I bump the fear factor up another notch in Yoon. His hand trembles as he mindlessly moves papers around his desk.

His phone sounds that he's received a text. He looks at it. From the PRK. For moments he stares, afraid to open it. He taps the icon of it. *Move ahead with university acquisition. Get everything in place now.*

Yoon sits perfectly still. He has a meeting scheduled with the university group overseeing the deal tomorrow morning. He will push them with an offer they can't refuse.

After that, what will happen? I project into him. I push the idea into his mind he will be gone. He freezes.

When his brain starts to work again, he taps on his keyboard to open the portal to the sensors in Leon's house. The cams are dark, the mics silent. Leon found them.

Could this day get any worse?

Chapter 66

"You know the people who set up this kill are still around, right?" asks Ginger as they're driving back.

I am with Leon as he stares at her. "I do."

"What are you going to do about them?"

"I'm pretty sure it was my boss."

"Why would he do that?"

Leon tells Ginger about the Extraction Program and the danger his knowledge of it poses to the Institute. Though Barbara knew the basics, this was new detail.

"That's pretty fucked up. So where do you stand with them now?" asks Ginger.

"With the university acquisition coming up, I'm supposed to clean up the basement tomorrow so there's no trace of the torture."

"And?" prompts Ginger.

"I think I'll go in as if nothing's happened and see what Yoon does."

"You don't think there's a danger?" asks Barbara.

"Yoon would never get his hands dirty, and an *accident* now would not help things along. With the university deal coming. I'll be safe." Leon's new phone rings. It's Jon.

"Jon, I'm sorry. Some things happened and I was unable to call. Are you okay?"

"Yeah. Are we meeting for lunch tomorrow?"

"Sure. I'll be there doing some work first thing tomorrow. How are things going?"

"We're getting guests from the university in the morning. It looks like this deal is moving ahead at the speed of light."

"I'll see you tomorrow. Get some rest."

Not sure that only one team was out to kill them, they head for the motel and a safe bed rather than home.

* * *

I am with Leon as he goes into work in the morning. After checking in at security, Leon heads downstairs. Dismantling the equipment isn't difficult, but where to put it afterward wasn't made clear to him. He decides to use the cells as storage rooms. At noon, he calls Yoon.

"Dr. Yoon, this is Leon." He hears a gasp. "I need some advice on storing the equipment down here. Could you come down after lunch?"

He can hear the tension in Yoon's voice. "I have meetings until two o'clock. I'll come down after that."

"Thank you, sir." Leon is chuckling as he calls Jon. "Meet me out front and we'll go to lunch."

"I'll check with Dr. Yoon."

"Don't bother. He's tied up in meetings. See you in a few minutes."

I'm with Leon and Jon. They drive to a sports bar known for its burgers. "No noisy kids today, Dad?"

"The guy tailing us won't be a problem today. We need to talk and it's quieter here."

Only three of the tables are occupied. Their booth is in the back. After the waitress drops off menus and waters, she leaves.

"I noticed the car is different. What happened, Dad?"

Leon relates the events from yesterday. *I feel Jon's surprise.*

"You killed them?"

"Shhh!" says Leon, looking around. Nobody's paying attention to them. "Technically, your aunt did, but yeah, the three of us set it up. It was us or them."

"What now?"

"To be honest, we're figuring it out ourselves. I'm cleaning out the evidence of the Extraction Program, but I don't know what's next. I need to talk to Yoon."

"You don't think he'll try again?"

"I've documented everything, along with photos. It's all in our storage unit. If anything happens to me, see that it goes to the press and the police."

"The rumor is Kwang was called back to another country," says Jon.

I had planted that in Jon.

"I think it was the People's Republic of Korea."

"How did you figure that out?"

"Dream."

Leon nods. "I've had some vivid dreams too. The latest one warned me about the assassins. I still believe you'll be safe here. Even though you know about the Extraction Program, I'm pretty sure the university will insist you remain with the Institute." He glances at a monitor showing a football game. "And Yoon likes you."

Jon frowns. "They'll want to study me. I'm not sure how I feel about that."

"I'll take care of Yoon and any threats, so be your own boss. If it gets to be too much, leave."

"I really like what I'm doing, helping people, ya know."

"I do. Hang in there."

Their burgers arrive.

* * *

At the Institute, Jon goes back to the patients, Leon goes to the basement. At two o'clock sharp, Yoon comes in.

He looks around, inspecting everything. "You've done a nice job of cleaning up."

"There's one room left. I'll show you."

I am in both Yoon and Leon.

They walk into the electroshock room. I can feel Yoon's discomfort. Tentatively, he approaches the table with the tiedown straps. I insert an image of me on the table into his mind. He pushes against my intrusion, but I prevail. I project the scene where I die. My body spasms. There is no gag and my screams fill his head. I feel him reel at the shock. He reaches out to the metal table to steady himself. A jolt of electricity seems to shoot through his body, causing him to jump. But he can't pull away.

I push an image of a white gossamer body floating up. He remembers the video. The current builds and his body jerks. I stop the illusions as he falls to the floor.

"Dr. Yoon, are you all right?" Leon asks as he helps him sit up. "What happened?"

I had put the same images in Leon's mind but not as forcefully. He knew what Yoon experienced.

Yoon was speechless.

Leon leans down, his face close to Yoon's.

"Doctor, I'll tell you what's going to happen. Everything that went on down here is documented. If anything happens to me or Jon, copies and the video tapes will go to the police and the press. Part of that information is the affiliation you have with the Peoples Republic of Korea and the plan to use a virus to extort money from governments round the world."

Yoon's face shows complete surprise. "How…how do you know of that?"

Leon ignores the question. "After this deal with the university, Jon and I will continue to work here. You will ensure we will be left alone."

A tear drops from Yoon's eye. "I will not be here to oversee that. My failure with the virus program will result in my recall as soon as the university takes charge. What I experienced here," he glances up at the table, "will be nothing compared to what will happen to me in Korea. Our Supreme Leader does not tolerate failure." He hangs his head, looking at the floor. "The men you disposed of were the only assets I had. I assume you did do that?"

Leon nods. "Couldn't happen to a more deserving bunch of guys. Who will replace you here?"

"The Institute will be fully transferred to the university. My great regret is I will not be here to watch Jon. He is something remarkable." With shaking hands, Yoon touches the table. Not feeling any current, he pulls himself to his feet and walks out on unsteady legs.

Back in his office, Yoon sips tea and stares at the vial in his hand. Inside is a tan capsule. It was to be used in case he was captured and questioned. *But not by his own people.* The pill is supposed to be painless and quick. The symptoms will be that of a heart attack.

He glances around his office a last time. Life was so good here.

If he goes back to Korea, he will reveal everything he knows. They will send agents after Jon and take him back to Korea to study like a new species of insect. Fortunately, Kwang knew little about Jon. He looks down at the pill, not in the vial now but in his hand. One last sigh and he picks up his cup of tea. The pill is bitter.

Chapter 67

The pull I feel to join that dimension is too strong to resist much longer. I firm up the conduit to Jon so he can establish it himself. It will take practice, but he knows what it feels like. The links I have to the physical world, specifically Jon and Leon are dissolving. In the end, the revenge I wanted was meted out by those responsible, with only a little of my influence. Was this how it was supposed to be? I take a last look at the thread that was Yoon. It is cut and the clear thread that was intertwined with his has ended.

I no longer care anyway. Jon, Leon, Elena, and the Institute will get along without me. Or not. Everything I was in contact with will work without me. I have no reason or desire to stay.

Like shedding my skin, I release myself, my ego, and leave it behind as I'm drawn into the realm of Knowledge. Peace suffuses through me.

I am no longer me.

I am we.

Author's Notes

To those of you who follow my blogs on my website: www.rlclaytonbooks.com and my posts on X, you will understand I had problems writing this book. It wasn't writer's block but something else.

I wear the persona of my characters as I write. Taking on the persona of the spirit of a dead person was difficult at first. I got used to it, and in fact enjoyed it. The realm after death was also hard at first. Years ago, I imagined it as "The Universe of Null." It is a place of no material…not solids, not liquids, not gas. It has no energies or forces as we have in the physical world. Nothing, except spirits. It is a place with no outside pressures or distractions. Imagining nothing is not easy.

The difficulty I had was the dimension of Knowledge. As my brain tried to take in the infinity of that place, it hurt. My mind is too small to conceive it. I would wake with headaches, and a dullness that took hours to put aside. Finishing the book is a satisfying relief.